"What will it take to make you forget me?"

"You're not a woman a man can easily forget," Dan said.

From the first time she'd met Dan again, she'd known she had to make a choice. A choice between the man whom, against all reason, she seemed to have fallen in love with, and the respectful life she'd made for herself.

She had to force herself to speak. "You must forget you ever met me."

She glanced at the desk—and realized the photo of her and her daughter was missing! She glanced wildly around the room.

"I assume you're looking for this." Dan drew the missing photograph from his tuxedo jacket.

Victoria stared at the photo and felt her world turn over.

"It isn't really me you've been afraid of all along," Dan went on. "You're afraid I'll find out I'm your baby's father."

Dear Reader,

Happy New Year! January is an exciting month here at Harlequin American Romance. It marks the beginning of a yearlong celebration of our 20th anniversary. Come indulge with us for twelve months of supersatisfying reads by your favorite authors and exciting newcomers, too!

Throughout 2003, we'll be bringing you some not-to-miss miniseries. This month, bestselling author Muriel Jensen inaugurates MILLIONAIRE, MONTANA, our newest in-line continuity, with *Jackpot Baby*. This exciting six-book series is set in a small Montana town whose residents win a forty-million-dollar lottery jackpot. But winning a fortune comes with a price and no one's life will ever be the same again.

Next, *Commander's Little Surprise*, the latest book in Mollie Molay's GROOMS IN UNIFORM series, is a must-read secret-baby and reunion romance with a strong hero you won't be able to resist. Victoria Chancellor premieres her new A ROYAL TWIST miniseries in which a runaway prince and his horse-wrangling look-alike switch places. Don't miss *The Prince's Cowboy Double*, the first book in this delightful duo. Finally, when a small Alaskan town desperately needs a doctor, there's only one man who can do the job, in *Under Alaskan Skies* by Carol Grace.

So come join in the celebrating and start your year off right—by reading all four Harlequin American Romance books!

Melissa Jeglinski
Associate Senior Editor
Harlequin American Romance

COMMANDER'S LITTLE SURPRISE
Mollie Molay

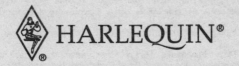

HARLEQUIN®

TORONTO • NEW YORK • LONDON
AMSTERDAM • PARIS • SYDNEY • HAMBURG
STOCKHOLM • ATHENS • TOKYO • MILAN • MADRID
PRAGUE • WARSAW • BUDAPEST • AUCKLAND

My thanks to Melissa Jeglinski
and my editor, Mavis Allen,
for their continued support.

ISBN 0-373-16954-X

COMMANDER'S LITTLE SURPRISE

Copyright © 2003 by Mollie Molé.

Visit us at www.eHarlequin.com

Printed in U.S.A.

ABOUT THE AUTHOR

After working for a number of years as a logistics contract administrator in the aircraft industry, Mollie Molay turned to a career she found far more satisfying—writing romance novels. Mollie lives in Northridge, California, surrounded by her two daughters and eight grandchildren, many of whom find their way into her books. She enjoys hearing from her readers and welcomes comments. You can write to her at Harlequin Books, 300 East 42nd St., 6th Floor, New York, NY 10017.

Books by Mollie Molay

HARLEQUIN AMERICAN ROMANCE

*Grooms in Uniform

Personal Connections

SWM 30, 6'2" blonde with blue eyes desperately seeking petite, twenty-something SWF for love and laughter. Are you the green-eyed, Baronovian beauty with whom I shared an unforgettable moonlit night of passion in the palace gardens last summer? Please let me know I wasn't dreaming! DOH ✉ ☎

Prologue

Dan O'Hara couldn't sleep. Jet lag had finally gotten the better of him.

Wide-awake, he paused in his pacing to gaze out the floor-to-ceiling palace windows at the manicured gardens that stretched into the distance. Under the dim light of the crescent moon, trees and bushes were decorated with streamers and lanterns in honor of the upcoming festivities. A three-tiered water fountain, in which tinkling cascades of water tumbled from the mouths of unicorns, occupied the center of the lawn. In the distance he caught sight of a well-tended maze. Nestled in its center was the silhouette of a white gazebo.

Dan blinked. If he didn't know better he would have thought that before him there was a fairy-tale setting in a fairy-tale country. He'd never even heard of Baronovia before his friend and fellow JAG lawyer, Commander Wade Stevens, had fallen in love with Duchess Mary Louise—better known to him as

May Baron. In two days he was to be the best man at their wedding.

He'd taken off his suit jacket and tie, and was starting to unbutton his shirt when drifting clouds passed over the moon. He was about to turn away when he caught a glimpse of a slight, shadowy feminine figure slip out of the palace. To his bemusement, she was wearing a filmy white robe and white slippers. Her long chestnut hair flowed freely down her back almost to her waist. Enchanted, he moved closer to the window and watched as she stopped to gaze up at the moon. Moments later she raised her arms over her head to the moon, twirled around, then lowered her arms to her chest. It looked as if she was trying to draw the moon down to her. He found himself smiling in sympathy at the gesture.

Whoever the woman was, she was beautiful, ethereal and intriguing. After a long plane flight and with probably a sleepless, empty night ahead, she seemed a damn good reason to stay awake.

It took him only a few seconds to make up his mind to join her.

Chapter One

The romantic atmosphere created by her cousin's wedding this weekend stirred Victoria Esterhazy's senses. At twenty-three, and with, as custom demanded, her own arranged marriage imminent, she yearned to experience a night of real love before it was too late. Certain she would be alone in these early-morning hours, she gave in to an impulse to dance away her romantic yearning under a new moon in the palace garden.

She bit back a gasp of dismay when a male figure materialized out of the night and strode toward her. Hugging her sheer robe about her body, she froze, ready to run.

"Are you real, or are you just a figment of my imagination?" he whispered as he came to her side.

Victoria shook her head. He might look like the romantic figure she'd conjured up in her head, but he was a stranger. What would happen if she were to be found here in the gardens in the middle of the night with him?

When she looked as if she was about to run, Dan began to feel foolish. His mystery lady had come out of the palace; she could be a member of the royal family. He was out of line, and he knew it, but somehow he didn't care, even if the last thing he needed was to offend a member of the bride's family. Whoever she was, she was entitled to her privacy. After all, he was no more than the best man at the wedding.

Dan knew he should go back to the palace and try to sleep, but he couldn't bring himself to leave... not just yet. There was something magical about her that drew him to her. Something that made him want to linger by her side.

She finally whispered, "Who are you?"

"A figure from your imagination—a phantom," he answered softly. There was no point in giving her his name, he thought. He had the strong feeling that they were living a fairy tale, and might never meet again after tonight. When she still lingered, he hesitantly gathered a few strands of silken hair that fell over her shoulders and let it fall through his fingers. "You have beautiful hair," he murmured, when she gazed wide-eyed at him. His gaze drifted lower to her lips. "Tell me, moon sprite, who are you?"

Victoria glanced back at the dark windows of the palace looming behind her and shook her head. She might yearn to experience the kind of love her cousin May had found during her state visit to the

United States, but she couldn't afford to give away her true identity. Not when it might embarrass her family. Aware of his sensuous gaze sweeping her, she drew the low neckline of her sheer robe more closely together and turned to flee back into the palace.

Dan reached to stay her. "Don't go," he murmured as he gave in to an impulse to brush the soft skin on her cheek. To confirm that she was real, he told himself, but he knew better. She *was* real, and in her sheer nightclothes looked to be the most desirable and enchanting woman he'd ever met.

He smiled his pleasure when she remained frozen in place. Her skin was as soft and velvety as a fragile rose petal, her scent sweet. "Since you might turn out to be someone out of a fairy tale," he added with a wry smile, "I suppose I could call you a fairy princess or my mystery lady."

The silence drew them together. Crickets chirping in the background and the water splashing down the tiered water fountain were the only sounds to break the stillness of the night. He was right, Dan thought as he gazed down at her. Under the dim light of the cloud-covered moon that shone over them, she did look like a figure out of a romantic fairy tale. To make matters even more intriguing, if not downright sensuous, the faint scent of gardenias clung to her.

Driven by a deep and unexpected emotion, Victoria felt herself responding to the yearning in her phantom's gaze. Her skin tingled, her heart beat faster and a glow spread throughout her middle. Soon to be married to an unknown man of her father's choice, she was all too aware no mere mortal man could have affected her so.

"If I'm your princess," she murmured shyly, "then you must be my phantom prince."

Her phantom was a tall, masculine man. His blond hair was tousled and his white shirt was partially unbuttoned as if he'd started to undress. After a closer look at his chiseled features, she found herself aching to explore his tanned skin just as he had touched hers moments before. She wanted to wind her fingers through the light, curly hair she'd glimpsed on his chest. To feel his arms around her and, heaven help her for her runaway thoughts, to taste his lips on hers.

Drawn to her phantom as if to a magnet, Victoria gazed into his warm blue eyes and the questioning smile that curved his lips. A thought came to her like a whisper out of the night; this man could be her destiny, sent to her by the gods she thought had passed her by. Hers, to have and to hold, if only for tonight.

Carried away by the crescent moon and the romantic setting, she gave in to the need to have him hold her, caress her, to make her his. To have, for at least a few precious moments in her life, a chance to create a memory to last her a lifetime. A memory of a love chosen by her for herself. Gazing into his warm blue eyes, she shivered at the thought of how it might feel to be held in his arms.

"Cold?" Drawn by the longing he saw in her eyes, Dan couldn't help himself. He put his arms around her shoulders and gathered her to him.

"Not anymore," she whispered a moment later when she burrowed closer into his warmth and closed her eyes. A moment later, his open shirt drew her gaze. Before she realized what she was about to do, she ran her fingers through the blond curls on his chest. It was the first time she'd touched a man so intimately, she thought as she felt the stirring of desire. "You make me warm all over."

Dan gasped as his body responded to her touch. Of all the things he might have expected to happen to him tonight, finding this enchanting woman in his arms and responding to his desire so honestly wasn't it.

He turned her chin up with a forefinger until their eyes met. He intended to give her one last chance to turn away, but the yearning he glimpsed in her blue-green eyes melted any reservations he might have had. They were two actors in a scene that had to be part of the fairy tale in the fairy-tale country he'd found himself in. Considering the rising mist and the surreal darkness surrounding them, he was half-afraid he was bound to wake up in the morning and find it had all been a dream.

Tomorrow would have to take care of itself, he decided as he drew her back into his arms.

He caressed her warm, silky skin and felt himself responding to the yearning in her eyes. Driven by an impulse that had come over him the moment he'd caught a glimpse of her dancing in the moonlight, he smiled down into her eyes. "I have to kiss you."

Kiss her? Victoria sensed that if she agreed to a kiss, one kiss would not be enough. Not for him, and certainly not for her. This was a moment like none other she'd experienced before in her sheltered life. Considering her pending arranged marriage, this might be a moment like none she would experience again. She nodded, raised her lips to his and put her arms around his neck.

She was right about the kiss, she thought; he held her so tightly her breasts were crushed against his chest. She moaned softly at the bittersweet pain.

"Sorry." He took a deep breath and held her away from him. "I didn't mean to hurt you."

Shaken by the magical sensations rushing through her, and sensing they were just a prelude, Victoria shook her head. "You haven't. Just love me."

"I will," he promised and lowered his head to hers. Gently, back and forth, his lips moved, teasing her lips into opening for him. When his tongue brushed the inside of her mouth as he deepened his kiss, Victoria's world tilted on its axis. When he moved on to her throat and down to the slant of her exposed breasts, she experienced shocks of sweet sensation. And when he lowered her gown and teased her sensitive nipples with his tongue, she melted in his arms.

She heard him sigh, felt his hands tighten around her, pulling her closer. "This may sound crazy, but I can't get enough of you," she heard him murmur. "*Who* are you, moon sprite? Where have you come from? Where can I find you in the morning?"

"It doesn't matter," she whispered. "We have tonight." She glanced around her, searching for a more private place where she could show him how real she was without revealing her identity. A place where the world couldn't intrude on her new-found happiness.

Tonight would be the night of passion she had dreamed of all her adult life, she mused as she slipped across the lawn, drawing her phantom lover with her. She would make love with him until the dawn, then slip away into the real world. For surely such a man could only exist in a dream.

Victoria drew him deep into the heart of the maze until they reached the white lattice-work gazebo. Cushioned benches rimmed the walls; luxurious rugs carpeted the floor and sweet-smelling vines crept through the latticework. "This used to be one of my favorite places to hide when I was a little girl and came to visit my cousin," she said happily. "I used to sit here hoping no one would find me, and I'd invent all kinds of fairy tales."

"And now?" He stroked the sides of her face with gentle hands. "Is it still your favorite place to hide?"

"Not since I grew up," she said, "but it is as long as you're here with me." She raised her lips for his kiss.

Her phantom lover murmured his pleasure at her answer. Grasping her around the waist, he drew her to a cushioned corner of the gazebo. He ran his hands over her shoulders, her swollen breasts that ached for his lips. And slowly, sensuously down her hips to the place that cried out for his touch. She couldn't get enough of him, couldn't wait to belong to him.

"Love me," she said impulsively, not recognizing herself. She felt alive, wanton and needy for him. Her hands plucked at his shirt until he drew it over his shoulders and, chest bare, pulled her into his arms again. She tongued his nipples as he had tongued hers and found his bare skin salty to the taste. Flames ran through her as her desire to become his grew. "Love me as if you mean it," she whispered.

"I do," he said into her lips, his voice shaking with desire. "So help us both, moon sprite, I do."

"My turn," he finally said and drew her robe and nightgown all the way off her shoulders. She stepped out of the garments and he tossed them onto a bench, held her away from him for a moment, then smiled. "You're even lovelier than I thought you would be."

In a few heated moments her phantom became everything she had wished for, dreamed of and had despaired of ever finding, Victoria thought dimly as she lost herself in a storm of passion. Skin to skin, lips to lips, he drew her deeper and deeper into a fantasy world that knew no end of desire. She forgot everything but the man who was making all of her yearnings come true.

"I love you," she heard herself whisper when her release began to ebb, leaving her floating in a warm sea of sensations. "I will love you forever," she whispered into his closed eyes.

Too late, she realized her phantom lover had drifted off to sleep. She smiled sadly as she realized he hadn't heard a word she'd said. She shouldn't complain, she told herself. After all, he'd taken her into a place every woman dreamed of. A place she'd longed to be in without knowing why.

And now she knew.

She moved closer into his warmth and closed her eyes. The return to reality would inevitably come with the dawn, but the night belonged to her.

CUDDLED UNDER the blankets in her room in the palace's guest wing later that day, Victoria opened her eyes when she heard her name. The lasting sweet sensations of last night's stolen hours still lingered. A new tender sensation between her thighs reminded her of last night's passionate embraces.

"Time to get up, my dear." Lydia Monsour, Victoria's long-time elderly friend and companion, glanced at the small gold watch pinned to her blouse. "It is well past noon."

"Not now, please," Victoria murmured, reluctant to let go of a dream that had come true.

"Now," Lydia said firmly. "Today is a very important day. The wedding rehearsal for your cousin's wedding is to take place this afternoon."

Victoria smiled dreamily. The romantic wedding ambience of her cousin's marriage had been part of the reason for her restlessness last night. A restlessness she wouldn't have been able to explain before, not even to herself. But now she knew it had been the desire of a woman to be held in the arms of a man who loved her back. Last night had turned into the most wonderful night of her life.

She glanced over at Lydia. If there were anyone she could tell of meeting her phantom lover last night without hearing recriminations, Lydia was the one.

"I met someone late last night," she began dreamily. "Out in the palace gardens."

Lydia froze. "Alone? At night? It isn't done! If you wanted to go out to get some fresh air, you should have called me. I would have gone with you."

"Yes, alone." Victoria stretched and turned over on her back. "He was wonderful."

"Obviously." Lydia glanced uneasily at her charge's glowing face. "Who was he?"

"An American. Probably one of the groomsmen over here for May's wedding."

Lydia relaxed. "Good. Then we don't have to worry about your meeting him again once the wedding is over. He will undoubtedly return home."

"I have to find him, Lydia," Victoria said. She threw back the covers. "First, I'm going to take a shower." Dream or not, real or not, and no matter what Lydia might think of her, Victoria had to find her phantom. "I have to know if last night was a dream or real."

Lydia tightened her lips. "I don't understand what drove you to do such an outrageous thing, my dear; certainly not after your convent upbringing. Did you stop to think of possible consequences?"

Victoria shook her head.

"I thought not," Lydia sighed. "Your mother has told me that your own wedding will be announced soon."

Victoria smiled. "Not when I tell her I have found the man I love."

"You said it was in the middle of the night. How will you be able to recognize the man in daylight?"

"I'll know him from the sound of his voice," Victoria said as she headed for the shower. "He has an American accent, the same as Cousin May's bridegroom. He must be here as a member of the groom's party. That should make it easy to find him.''

Lydia sniffed and hung up the dress Victoria had worn last night. "Easier said than done, my dear. Americans all sound alike to me. From what I hear, the groom has invited six of his fellow naval officers to serve as groomsmen. With the men in uniform, how will you be able to tell one from another?''

With her phantom's face in her mind's eye, his low, melodious voice still sounding in her ear, Victoria blew Lydia a kiss. "I'm sure I will be able to find him.''

Lydia smiled sadly and watched Victoria disappear into the bathroom. First as Victoria's childhood nanny, and now her close companion, she understood her charge all too well. Young blood, a royal wedding and a romantic, uniformed hero were a potent combination not easily cooled by a convent upbringing and the prospect of an arranged marriage. Victoria was no different than other young women of her age.

As she looked under the bed for Victoria's shoes, Lydia mulled over the coming wedding. May, Victoria's royal cousin, had managed to escape the stringent customs of the royal family as practiced in the twenty-first century, but there was a difference. This was to be May's second wedding, her first, an arranged marriage, having ended with her husband's untimely death.

As a member of the extended Baron family, Lydia knew that no matter how Victoria felt about the archaic custom, her charge's marriage, like May's first, would be determined by her father.

She muttered her dismay at what might happen if Victoria did somehow manage to find the man she'd encountered in the palace gardens last night. The only peaceful thought she had was in knowing that whoever the man had been, he would be gone forever in a matter of hours.

When Victoria returned, they were interrupted by a knock on the door. "Excuse me, ma'am," a palace footman said politely, "I have a message for Miss Esterhazy."

Victoria caught her breath. Was it possible her phantom lover had found her before she had a chance to find him? Her heart raced as she took the envelope Lydia handed her and tore it open. Seconds later, her face whitened.

"Something is wrong?" Lydia dropped Victoria's slipper on the bed and hurried to her side. "Have you had bad news?"

"My father wishes to see me. At once," Victoria murmured as she dropped the message to the floor. She glanced at her watch. "With the rehearsal only hours away, what could Papa possibly want that is so important?"

"Oh, dear! You don't suppose he knows about

last night, do you?'' Lydia shuddered. ''I blame my-self. It would never have happened if I had kept a closer watch over you.''

Victoria patted Lydia's ample shoulder. ''I'm a grown woman now, Lydia. Papa couldn't possibly know about last night. I'll tell you what Papa wants when I come back.''

Victoria squared her shoulders and made her way to a suite set aside for wedding guests. In spite of what she'd told Lydia, her thoughts were uneasy as she knocked on the door. ''Papa? You wished to see me?''

Basil Esterhazy, tall and stately, with the famous Baron cleft in his chin, smiled down at her. ''Come in. Come in and sit down, my dear. Your mother and I have good news to share with you.''

Victoria dutifully kissed her silent mother's cheek and took a seat on the velvet upholstered couch be-side her. ''Good news?''

''Yes.'' Her father beamed at her and cleared his throat. ''Weddings seem to bring out the romantic nature of people, do they not?''

Smiling, Victoria agreed as her thoughts flew to her mystery man and the precious hours they had spent together. ''Yes, Papa, I suppose they do.''

''With May getting married to her American suitor, it appears you are going to be the next bride in the family,'' he said as he gazed fondly at his only child.

''I am?'' A cold premonition passed over Victoria's shoulders. Her worst fears seemed about to be realized as her mother took her hand and squeezed it gently.

"Yes, my dear. Because you are our only child, I've put off arranging your marriage until now. However, you are now twenty-three. Accordingly, I have accepted Rolande Bernard's suit for your hand in marriage." He paused to let the announcement sink in. "You will no doubt be happy to know he wishes the marriage to take place as soon as arrangements can be made."

"Rolande Bernard?" Victoria's head swam, a hollow feeling grew in her middle. "He's much older than I am, Papa. I scarcely know him. Why would he wish to marry me?"

Her father frowned. "Bernard is a smart man. He recognizes your worth and your position in the family. We both agreed that the marriage will be an asset to our country and to him in his new position as our ambassador to the United States."

Victoria's mother, Clara, generally too docile for Victoria's own peace of mind, spoke up. Clad in a blue velvet cocktail suit for the upcoming wedding rehearsal, she put an arm around her daughter and frowned at her husband.

"As usual, Basil, you are being obtuse and thinking as a man. Our daughter wishes to know if Rolande cares for her, not that she will be an asset to him."

"Of course he does, or he wouldn't have asked

for her hand in marriage," her father huffed. "Furthermore, the reason he wishes to marry immediately is that he is about to present his credentials to the United States State Department. He will become Baronovia's first ambassador to the United States in a matter of weeks." He turned his annoyed gaze on Victoria. "Rolande feels, as I do, that at his side, you will make a fine showing for our country. I would remind you that it is your duty, Victoria."

Victoria nodded faintly. She'd always known that she would eventually marry the man of her father's choice. It had been that knowledge as well as the romantic wedding of her cousin to her American naval officer that had prompted her to accept her phantom lover last night. But now? Just when she'd tasted love, her world was about to fall apart.

"I would like to have time to think about this, Papa," she murmured.

Her mother patted her on her shoulder. "Not too long, my dear, your father wishes to make the announcement soon. All will be well, you'll see. Rolande Bernard may seem to be a little too old for you, but he is a fine man with a bright future. I'm sure you will be happy."

When Victoria managed a weak smile, her mother went on as if everything was settled. "You will enjoy living in the United States. And just think! Your cousin May will be living nearby."

Evading her father's frown, her dream of finding

her phantom lover in ashes, Victoria excused herself and made her way back to her suite. Her heart broken, Victoria wanted to hide from the world. May's wedding rehearsal, the following dinner and the wedding would have to go on without her.

Chapter Two

Eighteen Months Later

Victoria Esterhazy Bernard stood on the balcony overlooking the gardens of the new Baronovian embassy in Washington, D.C. Dusk had fallen; the bright lights around the perimeter of the embassy grounds had yet to come on. The scene, reminding her of the palace gardens in Baronovia, only added to her uneasiness.

Newly arrived in D.C. after a year spent with her husband in his diplomatic post in England, she was filled with pain, longing and loneliness at his unexpected demise in an automobile accident. The time in London hadn't brought her the happiness in her marriage she had hoped for. The only bright light in her life was her baby daughter, Caroline.

She glanced at the card inviting her to her cousin's housewarming one more time. If ever there was an invitation to disaster, this had to be it, she thought sadly. What if she accepted the invitation and ran into the man with whom she'd shared that forbidden night in the garden almost two years ago? Even now she knew nothing about him other than that he'd been an American and a friend of the groom.

What she did know was that as the widow of Baronovia's ambassador to the United States and her appointment to the position herself, she couldn't afford to be involved in a scandal. Especially when the suspicious circumstance surrounding her husband's death remained unexplained. She sighed and handed the card to her long-time friend and companion, Lydia Monsour.

Lydia read the engraved invitation. "At last," she said slowly. "If your cousin's American friends are invited, you will be able to solve the mystery that has plagued you. You might find Caroline's father."

Victoria wandered around the room, listlessly picking up and discarding her hairbrush, her comb. "What good would it do? I'm a widow now with a diplomatic position to uphold."

"At least you would know the man's name."

Victoria shook her head. "It would only cause more heartache. Rolande was my husband and therefore my baby's father."

Lydia clucked sympathetically as she handed back the invitation. "You've been hiding in the embassy since we arrived here. Go. Your cousin May will be unhappy if you don't show up."

"I hesitate to go to the party so soon after Rolande's death."

Lydia paused and peered over her glasses. "If you keep a low profile, everything should be fine. Unless you've forgotten your phantom. Have you?"

Victoria shrugged as if it didn't matter, but inwardly she knew she still cared for the man. How could she forget the man who had taught her what it meant to be a woman? To fall in love.

How could she forget the bittersweet memories of the man who had changed her life forever?

"Go, my dear," Lydia said quietly. "You will never know peace until you do."

Victoria reached for the large quilted bag that had become part of her wardrobe. "He didn't try to find me in Baronovia, why would he care to see me now? Besides," she said with a shiver, "what if he doesn't want to remember me? What if our night together never meant anything to him?"

"He didn't find you because once your father told you he'd arranged your marriage, you didn't want to be found," Lydia reminded her. "Once you see the man again, you can close the book on the past."

"I can't, Lydia. It would only break my heart."

"So you still care for this man?"

Victoria smiled sadly. "More than you'll ever know," she said softly, as if to herself. "But the fact remains, that whoever he was then, or whoever he is now, he is forever out of my reach."

* * *

WHEN Lieutenant Commander Dan O'Hara entered the headquarters of the U.S. Navy Judge Advocate General Corps, it was abuzz with excitement over a newspaper account of the upcoming party that had been pinned to the office bulletin board. It wasn't every day a member of the JAG corps married a European duchess, he heard someone say. Or that he had brought her home to set up housekeeping in the United States.

Dan stopped to glance at the newspaper clipping. He had received an engraved invitation for the party. Wade and May Stevens had also invited the JAG and his staff to celebrate the purchase of their first home in the United States.

Lieutenant Lester Howard whistled as he glanced over O'Hara's shoulder. "To tell you the truth, sir, I wouldn't have bet a nickel the commander's marriage would have lasted this long. After all, his wife is a duchess and Stevens was her bodyguard."

The comment, uttered into a sudden silence, quickly drew an audience. To his dismay, a dozen pairs of eyes focused on Dan.

Dan shrugged. The Stevenses' courtship had had its ups and downs in the early stages when Wade had been the duchess's bodyguard. But judging from the look on their faces, things have never looked better. "Why not?"

"Heck, his wife is a duchess, that's why. How's she going to settle for living like the rest of us?"

"Maybe because Stevens saved her life," Dan said dryly as he turned to go to his office.

"It's just like a fairy tale," Lieutenant Linda Kimball, the junior officer in charge of administrative affairs, said enviously. "You were the best man at their wedding, weren't you, sir?"

"Right." Dan took a last look at the invitation and headed for his office. Just remembering his stay in Baronovia and the woman he'd met at the Stevens wedding made his body warm and his heart ache. He might have come up empty when he'd tried to find her before he left, but forget her? Never.

"Wait up a minute, sir," Howard called after him. "So what's a real palace like?"

A barrage of questions filled the air.

Dan tried to focus on Howard's question. He thought of the ornate guest room with its lush wine-colored velvet drapes, upholstered furniture to match and the lace curtains at the windows. There had been a bed large enough for a family of four to sleep in. And a portrait of a dour Baron ancestor that had looked down on him from over the large fireplace where a fire smoldered. As luxurious as the setting had been, he hadn't been able to sleep.

A glance out the window had taken him outside to a woman he would never, in this lifetime, forget.

"Nice, but formal and a little intimidating," he finally answered. "I couldn't wait to get home where I can put my feet up and have a cold beer."

"What's the duchess like?" Linda Kimball asked wistfully. "Is she as beautiful as they say?"

"Let's just say she's not like the girl next door," Dan said wryly. He waved off any more questions and backed into his office.

What continued to surprise him after all this time was that eighteen months later he still thought about the ethereal woman he'd encountered in the Baronovia palace gardens. He'd wondered on and off why he hadn't been able to find her the next morning. Maybe, he thought as he stared into his blank computer screen, she *had* been just a dream.

A burst of laughter outside Dan's open door distracted him. He glanced up in time to see a female junior officer being kissed under a giant spring of mistletoe left hanging after the recent office Christmas and New Year's parties.

Cheered on by laughing bystanders, the kiss was lasting longer than Dan thought necessary. To make him really uncomfortable in his nostalgic state of mind, the kiss served to remind him of a night that, by all logic, he should have forgotten long ago.

He wasn't a ladies' man, but he hadn't been a hermit, either. His mystery woman hadn't been the only woman in his life, but she was the one he couldn't forget.

There had been something so special about her that he had searched for her among the guests. On the chance she was a member of the bridal party, he looked for her during the wedding rehearsal and at the dinner that followed. To add to his frustration, the pomp and circumstance of the wedding had prevented him from actively searching for her. He couldn't have exactly asked if anyone knew a woman of her description; young with long, auburn hair and a body that had been made to fit in his arms, could he?

"Commander?" A knock on the open door broke into Dan's reverie.

It was Howard again. "Sorry to bother you, sir, but we were trying to decide what kind of gift would be appropriate for the commander's housewarming. We figure it has to be something special for someone like the duchess."

"Suit yourself. I'm planning on giving them a toaster." He motioned for Howard to close the office door so he could get back to work.

Instead of opening the file on his desk, Dan decided it was time to get his mind off the past. He needed to map out his New Year's resolutions and stick to them. And they didn't include daydreaming about a woman who might not have been real. Who, if she had been real, hadn't been interested in seeing him again.

With a last look through the glass door of his office at the celebration going on outside, Dan turned on his computer and drew up his first New Year's resolution. After all, he told himself with a glance at the waiting file, it had to be smarter to plan for the future than to wait for his future to come to him. A methodical man by nature, he spent the next half hour drawing up a five-year plan.

Bottom line, he mused when he finally checked the printout of his plan and closed down his computer, he was in his thirtieth year and it was time to settle down. Ergo, he would marry when he turned thirty-five and have two children by the time he was forty—that is, if his wife were willing. At that age he would be old enough to choose a wife wisely. As for children, he assured himself as he mentally flexed his arm muscles, he would still be vigorous enough to play baseball without looking like a complete fool.

In retrospect, he should have known fate had a way of laughing at the plans of a mere mortal man.

TWO WEEKS LATER, Dan stood on the doorstep and admired the Stevenses' new address. The redbrick house on the outskirts of D.C. had green-and-white shutters and showed its distinguished lineage.

Bushes flanking the green doorway were lit with ropes of tiny bright lights. A welcome sign hung over a large wreath of apples, pears and pinecones woven with red and green ribbons and giving off a tart, sharp scent. As he started up the steps, music and laughter drifted through the open windows.

Dan grinned and crossed his fingers. With both the duchess and Mike Wheeler's wife, Charlie, present tonight, he hoped the evening would go without a mishap. Or if it didn't, that he wouldn't be asked to help clear it up. He'd already been chewed out by Admiral Crowley, the JAG, for getting involved with the duchess's and Charlie Wheeler's life-threatening problems. The memory of Crowley's flashing eyes and hard language on both occasions still stung.

His friend Wade Stevens had eventually married his duchess, and Mike his free-spirited concierge, but Dan intended to stay clear of anyone even associated with Baronovia.

Relieved to find the door guarded against unwelcome visitors, he handed over his invitation and sauntered inside.

To the left of the entry hall was a room filled with guests. Waiters were circulating with trays of hors d'oeuvres and champagne. To his right, a large room with a polished wooden floor had been cleared of furniture to make room for dancing couples. A string trio was playing in a corner.

"O'Hara! Over here." Wade Stevens motioned Dan to join him. Dan nodded and made his way through the crowd.

Pretty as a picture in her short black cocktail dress with a single diamond hung on a slender gold chain at her throat, Wade's petite royal wife held out her hand. "We are so happy to have you and all of our friends here to help us celebrate our good fortune. The night is wonderful, no?"

"Wonderful, yes," Dan agreed, amused at the way her syntax still remained old-country. It was a habit that endeared the duchess to everyone who met her.

"I have someone I would like you to meet." May smiled and looked over his shoulder. "My cousin Victoria. Have you met her?"

"Sorry. I'm afraid I wouldn't recognize her if I did."

"Are you sure you didn't meet her at my wedding?"

Puzzled by May's question when he'd already disclaimed recognizing her cousin, Dan turned back. "Not that I remember. Maybe I wasn't paying attention when we were introduced."

May smiled at him over the rim of her glass. "I'll introduce you."

"I'll look forward to it," Dan said politely. Whatever the reason for May's questions, he wasn't particularly interested. "If you don't mind, I could use a drink," he said with a smile. "See you later."

Dan made his way around the room to the bar and refreshment tables, stopping now and again to say hello to someone he knew. If he were lucky, he mused as he reached for a cold beer, May's cousin Victoria wouldn't show up. The last person he cared to meet was a member of the duchess's family. May, at least, behaved like a normal woman, but most royals were a pain in the rear. Meeting this one would be a waste of time.

He was in the midst of choosing from an eye-catching tray of appetizers when May Stevens came up behind him and tapped him on the shoulder.

"I've found her. Dan, I would like you to meet my cousin Victoria. Vicky, this is Dan O'Hara."

Dan thanked the waiter and motioned the tray away. "Pleased to meet you," he said as he turned around—then froze. One look into her blue-green eyes and a moment of déjà vu broadsided him. "I'm sorry... I know you, don't I?"

To his surprise, she tensed and took back her extended hand. "I don't think so."

Dan looked to May for help. May shrugged and looked just as puzzled as he felt. He was on his own. "Perhaps we met at your cousin's wedding last year?"

"Perhaps," she answered, still tense.

Dan shook his head to clear the cobwebs that muddled his thoughts. He returned Victoria's apprehensive gaze and felt his heart thud in his chest. The atmosphere surrounding them turned heavy. The sound of music and voices faded into the background.

This was a different time and a different place, he told himself. In her white silk dress and short, cropped blond hair, the woman gazing back at him looked familiar, but he wasn't sure where and when they'd met.

He'd only met one woman before tonight who had had such an immediate effect on him. An exquisite woman with expressive eyes and a spirit that had caught at his heart the moment he'd glimpsed her from the palace window.

Was this the woman he'd met in the deep of night and made love to in Baronovia? And why was she so frightened?

He sure couldn't ask her such intimate questions with her cousin watching them and surrounded by dozens of people.

He cleared his throat and tried to recall the image of his mystery woman on that magical night. She'd had flowing waist-length auburn hair, so soft it had slipped through his fingers like silk. May's cousin had blond hair and it was cropped short in the irregular lengths so popular today.

As for her figure, his mystery woman had been so slender he'd been able to span her waist with two hands. Tonight's woman not only had fuller breasts, there were subtle differences in the rest of her body. If it were possible, she looked more womanly and more attractive than the woman he remembered.

"No, sorry. I guess not," he finally answered when the silence grew too long to be comfortable. "If we'd met before this, I'm sure we both would have remembered it.

As he spoke, he noticed an expression of relief cross her features. But not before he also caught a passing flash of regret.

Whatever was going on inside her, this Victoria's stiff body language didn't compute.

He recalled an announcement he'd heard last year

at May's wedding. If this was the same cousin, she'd been engaged to a future Baronovian ambassador. If the memory was true, and even if this was the same woman, she was untouchable.

He didn't know whether to be relieved or sorry. It was damn hard to let go of the memory of his mystery woman.

"Something to drink?" he said when May smiled and drifted away, leaving her cousin behind. Even though he and Victoria were alone now, there was no way was he going down the prickly path of asking her if she had been the woman he'd held in his arms and made passionate love to one night long ago.

"No, thank you," she answered softly. "I don't drink anymore."

Anymore? Dan glanced at his companion. If there was ever a word that called for a question and an answer, *anymore* was it. He started to speak, but there was something about the way her clear eyes regarded him that kept him from asking. His turn to find out more about her would surely come before the night was over. "How about a Perrier and maybe something to nibble on?"

"Yes, thank you."

Dan thought of his companion as he made his way to the bar. There was something odd about the way she kept avoiding looking at him. He'd be damned if he could pass up the opportunity to find out if she was his mystery woman without at least trying. He couldn't come right out and ask her, but there *was* one way he could discover the truth.

"Care to dance?" he asked after she'd silently sipped the drink he brought her. "Unless you've given up dancing, too?"

She hesitated. "No. I love to dance. I'm just not in the mood."

"Come on," he coaxed. "Just one dance?"

"Just one," she answered. "Then I have to leave."

Dan put their drinks on a tray held by a passing waiter, put his hand under her elbow and led her across the hall to the dance floor.

The answers to his question were going to add up without him even asking.

He knew she'd been at the palace the night before Wade Stevens had married his duchess.

She'd admitted to loving to dance.

The first time he'd laid eyes on his mystery woman, she'd been dancing her heart out.

Those clues had to mean something, Dan thought as he took her in his arms. At the same time, he couldn't help wondering why she looked as if she wanted to run.

Their encounter that night in the palace gardens had been a natural encounter between a man and a woman. She'd been a woman so beautiful, he'd gone down to her to see if she were real. When he'd taken her in his arms, felt her vibrant body and tasted lips as sweet as honey, he'd been lost.

He'd been attracted to that woman, and he was attracted to this one. As he held her in his arms, all his senses told him the woman he remembered was the same woman he was holding in his arms tonight.

If this Victoria did turn out to be her, he silently vowed, he'd take it from there. If not, one dance to be polite, an apology, and he'd find a way to be out of here.

He gazed in wonder at Victoria's blond hair and tried to envision her as a brunette. Outside of the difference in hair coloring and her more womanly figure, she had to be the same woman.

Maybe his mystery woman had a double.

Maybe…then again, he wondered, how could he account for the same, familiar faint scent of gardenias that clung to the woman in his arms?

Chapter Three

When Dan O'Hara took her into his arms, Victoria's heart skipped. The very meeting she'd feared had happened and her worst fears had come true. Not only had she found her phantom lover tonight here at her cousin's housewarming, she now found herself in the last place she should be if she had any sense—in his arms! There was no doubt in her mind that Dan was the man who had made love to her on that magical night eighteen months ago. Even then, with the afterglow of his embraces lingering long after she'd left him and gone back to the palace, she had thought he could be her destiny. Instead, he was dangerous.

"Enjoying yourself?" Dan asked.

"Thank you, yes. But I do have to leave." Even as she spoke, she prayed for the music to stop long enough for her to excuse herself to her cousin and leave.

"Too bad," he said, and signaled the band leader

to go on. "It would be a shame to waste such beautiful music."

As she automatically followed Dan's footsteps across the dance floor, thoughts ran through her mind as swiftly as a cold wind blows on a March day. No matter how sweetly her cousin May had begged her to come here tonight when she'd called to decline the invitation, she should have listened to her heart.

Tonight, from the moment he'd started to speak, she'd recognized Dan as her phantom lover. She'd tried but she'd never forgotten the sound of his deep, melodious voice with a hint of teasing laughter in it. No other man's eyes had warmed her so—a lifetime ago—and now again. And now that she was in his arms again, to her dismay she remembered his gentle strength and the taste of his lips.

It would never do. As the widow of a diplomat and Baronovia's new ambassador to the United States, she had to keep up appearances. Any hint of scandal could bring shame on her family.

Maybe it had been different for Dan. Maybe she'd been one of the many woman in every port that seamen were known to boast about. Had she only been a diversion, a pleasant way to spend a sleepless night?

Held in Dan's arms, Victoria remembered his earlier embrace, the taste of his lips, the sound of his voice murmuring words of assurance as he made love to her. And the way she had never been able to put him out of her mind.

She fervently prayed he wouldn't start to ask questions for which she couldn't give answers. At the same time, she had to bite her lip to keep from asking questions of her own.

If their encounter had meant something to him, why hadn't he tried to find her after their magical encounter, she wondered as she averted her face and forced a smile at a passing couple.

The music changed to a two-step, to the same romantic melody she'd hummed to herself when she'd danced alone in the palace garden that long-ago night. The night she had known true love for the first and only time in her life.

She closed her eyes and instinctively leaned into the arms that had once held her so possessively, so lovingly. Leaned into the arms that reminded her of stolen tender moments under a crescent moon, embraces that had awakened her pent-up desires long dreamed about and never experienced again.

Arms that reminded her of a night of rapture that had ended too soon.

To her growing dismay, Dan began to gently caress the small of her back. She shivered as electricity followed the path where his warm hand had passed. When he swept her across the dance floor, his hand on her bare skin sent mental images of tangled limbs, heated kisses. Bursts of unwanted raw sensation ran through her.

In spite of her misgivings, Victoria found herself softly humming the song's haunting lyrics under her breath, reliving the moments when she'd danced on a grass carpet under a moonlit sky. For a moment she was happy again, until he spoke.

"You may think I'm a little crazy, but you remind me of someone who..." Dan began softly. He needed time. Time, with Victoria in his arms. He'd been puzzled when they were first introduced, but he was pretty sure now she was his mystery woman.

His voice trailed off before he started again. "The truth is that when I saw you I happened to remember a night when I saw a woman dancing alone in the moonlight."

Wordlessly, Victoria gazed up at Dan. To her dismay, she remembered that same night too well. She couldn't admit being that woman even if she had wanted to. The time for the two of them to reveal themselves had passed long ago.

"Are you usually so quiet?" he finally asked with a smile and a quirked eyebrow. "Or am I boring you?"

Boring her? Not when the friction of his hand brushing across her bare back and the warmth of his hard body against hers were sending jolts of desire running through her.

Her mind in turmoil, Victoria couldn't speak. The woman he spoke of was gone. Victoria was a widow and a mother now. Besides, if she *were* free to admit

who she had been on that night, what would he think
of her?

"Victoria?"

No matter what she remembered, or how she felt
about Dan, she knew the past had to be forgotten.
She knew she had to get away from Dan, now, tonight and forever.

"Victoria?" he repeated, obviously puzzled at her
silence. "Are you all right?"

"I'm sorry," she finally answered. "I'm afraid
my mind was a million miles away."

"Ahh." To her dismay, he smiled down at her.
"To a palace garden in Baronovia? Maybe even to
a crescent moon and a vine-trimmed white gazebo?"

Victoria drew back. But not before Dan saw the
vein at the side of her throat began to throb visibly.

"I don't know what you are talking about," she
answered. To his chagrin, she looked as if she was
about to pull out of his arms and leave him alone
on the crowded dance floor.

"I was hoping you might remember," he went on
before she could make up her mind to leave. "After
holding you in my arms here tonight, I was silly
enough to think you were the woman I met in Baronovia over a year ago."

Dan gazed at Victoria when she remained silent.
Could he have been mistaken about her, after all?

When she shook her head again, he finally gave
up and set his mind to the music. What made tonight

so puzzling was that he kept thinking that no other woman could have been made to fit so perfectly into his arms like this woman. No other woman could have made such tender, yet such passionate, love with him that night so long ago. Nor had he ever forgotten her beautiful and expressive eyes that revealed her deepest thoughts, just as they were doing now.

If she wasn't his mystery woman, why was she so reluctant to look at him? "Did I say something to offend you? If I did, I'm sorry."

"No!" she said firmly. "It's just that I don't know what you're talking about. I've already told you, you have the wrong woman."

Dan wasn't prepared to give up, not yet. And certainly not when every one of his clamoring senses told him Victoria could be the very woman she'd denied being. Why else had he felt her heart beat wildly against his chest a moment ago? And why had she stiffened when she'd realized she'd actually allowed herself to melt into his arms?

He was about to apologize again when Victoria pulled out of his arms and rushed through the French doors onto an outdoor patio. Tables and chairs had been set out to accommodate guests. A crescent moon hung overhead, just as it had almost two years ago. An omen, he thought as he caught up with Victoria.

"Hold up! Was it something I said?" Dan asked when he caught up with her. "All I really meant to say was that you remind me of someone who meant a lot to me.''

"I'm sorry I've disappointed you, but I've already told you I'm not the woman you are looking for.'' She took a step away from him. "It is true my home *was* in Baronovia, but I haven't lived there for some time.''

Dan looked into her expressive eyes and at lips that were surely meant to be kissed. Desire ran through him. Victoria might not be his mystery woman, but he was as attracted to her as he had been to her double. He had to kiss her.

"Don't go, stay here with me,'' he said. He couldn't hold off any longer. Not only for the proof she and the woman he remembered were one and the same, but for the kiss he ached to take from her tantalizing lips.

He held her face in his hands and lifted her face to his. "Victoria,'' he whispered when their eyes met. "I'm not sure if you were the woman in the palace garden that night or not, but I'm still hooked. I can't seem to get enough of you.''

"What are you doing?'' Victoria gasped as she tried to pull out of his grasp. "I...''

"I only want to show you how I feel,'' Dan said, his lips only inches away from hers. "I have a feeling that tonight has to be one of the most important nights of our lives.''

He was prepared for her anger, but he wasn't prepared for the stricken look that came into her eyes.

He should have known she was too vulnerable to try to seduce into a confession. "How can I make it up to you for being so rude?" he said against her sweet-smelling hair—hair that was shorter and lighter than the auburn tresses of the woman he remembered, but just as beautiful.

"Victoria," he murmured when he couldn't wait any longer. "Victoria," he said again. "Look at me. Look at me and tell me the truth. Tell me you don't want me to kiss you."

Slowly, as if she were reluctant to answer him, let alone have him kiss her, Victoria ran her tongue over her dry lips. "What… What did you say?"

"Only this." He held her head between his hands and slowly lowered his mouth to hers. "You were meant to be kissed tonight—let it be me," he murmured as their lips met.

To her dismay, Victoria felt a surge of desire at the pull of his lips. His warm breath was tinged with the pungent scent of wine, his tongue eager to invade her mouth. The tender look in his eyes as he gazed at her and the hands that tightened around her waist as he drew her closer to him were too magnetic for her to deny. Reality vanished as Dan drew her deep, deep and still deeper into a sea of sensuality.

She fought the desire to loop her arms around his neck and kiss him with all the frustrated passion pent up inside her. How could she continue to deny him when she had yearned for him so long?

Would she be admitting she was his mystery woman if she did kiss him? More important, how could she continue to deny herself the truth? She had unwittingly fallen in love with him long ago and, heaven help her, she was in love with him now.

Just as Dan moved on to the sensitive place between her breasts, Victoria heard a small voice whisper caution in her ear.

She whimpered a protest, placed her hands on Dan's chest and pushed herself out of his embrace. She'd gone down that exciting, sensuous path eighteen months ago, but she couldn't afford to go down that road with him again. Not only for her sake, but for her daughter's.

Dan sensed Victoria's emotional withdrawal. He ached to kiss her again and yet again, but the anxious look in her eyes stopped him. Reluctant to let her go, he murmured a protest and held her against him long enough for his arousal to pass.

"Under the circumstances," he said wryly, "it might be wiser to keep my distance from now on, but right now I need a moment or two."

"Well?" he finally said softly. "Now do you remember me?"

Victoria shook her head and touched her lips with trembling fingers. "No. I'm still convinced you have the wrong woman."

"Coward." He gently outlined her lips with his thumb. "Is it because you really don't remember me? Or is it that, for some reason, you're afraid to admit it?''

Victoria shook her head. "I still don't know what you're talking about," she said, distracted by the yearning in Dan's eyes but firm in her resolve to keep him from guessing the truth.

"Victoria! There you are!" Wade Stevens called through the French doors. "Lydia just called. She's worried that your first social outing since your husband died is going okay. I told her you were fine."

Dan clasped his hands behind him to keep from reaching for Victoria again. "Why didn't your cousin introduce you as a married woman?"

Victoria shrugged to hide the way her heart was breaking at the reminder she had been married to the late Rolande Bernard. "It was only a social introduction. There was no need to tell you I have recently been widowed."

He looked shocked, but there was no other way to get him to back off and leave her alone.

Dan knew he had to let Victoria go. A recent widow, he had no right to be attracted to her. Even if it was damn clear he was on the verge of falling head over heels for her again. She not only didn't fit into his five-year plan, she was part of royal family. Wade, he thought again, had been lucky in his choice of a wife, but he didn't intend to take the same chance.

But what did bother the hell out of him was that he was jealous of a deceased man.

"Under the circumstances, it was gracious of you to come here tonight." He tried but he couldn't keep the disappointment out of his voice.

"It's more of a family thing. I didn't want to disappoint May, so I came here tonight."

She straightened the neckline of her dress, smiled politely and turned away to leave. But not before she paused a long moment and glanced back at him.

Shivers ran up and down Dan's spine again as he read the unhappy message in her eyes. She was trying to tell him they would never meet again.

He was sure Victoria had been about to say something to him before she left. Instead, there had only been that brief flash of sadness in her eyes before she disappeared through the French doors.

Dan's mental antenna tingled. He was ready to stake his life on the fact that she was hiding her true identity. She had to be afraid of admitting they had been together.

Afraid? God, he thought and raked his fingers through his hair. Why would she be afraid of him? All he'd wanted to do was to prove she had been the woman he'd made love to in Baronovia. To show her how much he'd cared for her then and even now.

Widow or not, he made up his mind not to let her leave before she told him why she had looked at him that way. Muttering to himself, he made his way through the ballroom and across the hall. Waiters were still passing trays of canapés, champagne was flowing freely and May Stevens was greeting late-comers. He drew her aside.

He'd never been the kind of man to mince words and he didn't intend to start now. "Sorry, duchess, I know you set me and your cousin up, no…don't deny it. What I want to know now is, why. And when you're finished explaining, I would like you to tell me where Victoria has disappeared to!"

May looked surprised. "I don't know what you mean. I only thought that since Victoria was here tonight without an escort, you could keep her amused."

Dan wasn't satisfied, but he wasn't prepared to force the issue. This was, after all, May's home and Victoria was her cousin.

"I don't know where she is now," May went on as she looked around the room. "She didn't say goodbye. Why don't you ask Wade?"

Dan eyed May's flushed features suspiciously. "That's it?"

"Of course. Victoria is a widow. I was only trying to make her feel at home."

Dan apologized, then headed over to Wade, who was busy helping tend the bar. When he got close enough to be heard over the noise, he leaned over the bar and asked, "Do you know where Victoria is? She's disappeared."

Wade shrugged and poured a whiskey on ice. "Beats me. Have you asked May?"

"Yep. Unfortunately, May says she's clueless,"

Dan answered dryly, "but between me and you, I have my doubts."

"Tried the ladies' room?

Whatever May might have known of the reasons for Victoria's disappearance, Wade wasn't in on it. Dan shook his head.

Wade poured a beer for another guest and wiped his hands on a towel. "My guess is Vicky was tired and went home."

Dan nodded and turned away. He had no right to ask any more questions, or to go after Victoria.

Maybe she hadn't been his mystery woman after all.

THERE WAS a light knock on Victoria's bedroom door. She lay curled up in the center of her bed, a book lying unread beside her. She glanced at the clock on the nightstand. "Come in, Lydia."

Lydia entered her bedroom. "I saw your light under the door, my dear. I wanted to say good-night."

Victoria smiled sadly. Dear Lydia seemed to know how much she missed her husband. He had been almost thirty years older than her. Rolande had had steel-gray hair at his temples and a trim body of a much younger man. A twentieth-century man in the twenty-first century, he had been courtly and respected. "You don't have to have permission to enter my bedroom, Lydia. You know you're always welcome here."

Lydia smiled. "I know. I just didn't want to disturb you. I wanted to see if you had actually fallen asleep with the light on.''

"I was only thinking," Victoria said.

"Of Rolande?"

"Yes."

Lydia smiled sadly. "How could I forget such a fine man? It is a shame he had to die under such circumstances.''

Victoria studied Lydia and sensed it hadn't only been the light that had attracted her. There was a questioning expression on her dear face. She stirred uneasily. "Is there something wrong?"

Lydia laughed. "I was about to ask you the same question, Vicky. You know me too well.''

"As you seem to know me. What is it?"

"I am still troubled by your reaction to the invitation to your cousin's housewarming. I also noticed you appeared unhappy when you returned home.'' Lydia paused and studied her for a long, deep moment. "You look disturbed now, my dear. Did you meet someone tonight out of your past?"

Victoria smiled ruefully. "How did you guess?"

"I'm no fool, Vicky. Only such a meeting could have left you looking so unhappy." Lydia studied her for a long moment. "You haven't forgotten your bargain with Rolande, have you?"

Victoria bravely met Lydia's gaze. They had always been honest with each other. She would be honest now.

"No, of course not. Rolande meant too much to me."

Lydia hesitated, then went on. "I also would like to remind you how important it is you let someone know if there is a problem."

Although she smiled her agreement, Victoria felt guilty when she recalled the way she'd reacted when she'd been introduced to Dan. "I know. As I said a moment ago, you know me too well. The meeting tonight meant nothing to me."

"Then, you have nothing to fear, Vicky," Lydia said. "Just remember, you've always had me to watch over you. Even now."

"I know, and I love you all the more for it," Victoria replied. "You've always been more than a friend to me."

Lydia nodded. "Then I will say good-night, my dear. Sleep well."

Victoria sank back against her pillows. If Rolande had been alive, she would have asked him to stay the night with her. She would have thrown back the bedcovers and invited him to join her. To stay and hold her in his arms. He had always made her feel so safe.

Victoria closed her eyes. If Rolande *had* been able to make love with her, she would have welcomed him. Instead, they both had had to be satisfied with their situation and with the strong bond they'd forged between them.

Her thoughts turned pensive.

She had discovered, and only by chance, that her anxious parents had arranged her marriage to Rolande because he had been a man old enough and wise enough to ensure her safety and happiness in a world that, in their opinion, had gone awry as proven by her cousin's marriage to an American naval officer.

When she had come to Rolande with the truth before their wedding, he had been honest with her. He, too, had a secret to share. They would do well together, he'd told her as they made their bargain. Impotent, a child to carry on his name had been his dearest wish.

There was no way she would betray the trust Rolande had placed in her.

Chapter Four

In the morning, Victoria awoke to find sunlight streaming through the lace curtains on the bedroom windows. The distant sound of a vacuum cleaner outside the door told her she'd overslept.

She'd been exhausted from worrying over her reaction to meeting Dan O'Hara again.

Poor Rolande, she mused guiltily as she turned over and stared at the carved ceiling above the bed. Even knowing he hadn't been able to meet her needs, he'd always tried to be kind and compassionate. He'd deserved so much more from her than her gratitude then. Even in death he deserved her loyalty.

How loyal could she be to his memory when she wasn't able to put her long-ago encounter with Dan in the past where it belonged? How loyal could she be when just the memory of Dan's tongue tracing her lips and his hands stroking her breasts caused molten heat to engulf her?

A knock on the door saved her from her runaway erotic thoughts. She glanced at the clock on her nightstand. It was long past the time when she was usually up and around. "Come in, Lydia!"

Her long-time companion entered the room carrying Caroline, Victoria's baby daughter. To Victoria's dismay, tears had formed in the baby's velvety blue eyes. One look at her mother and the baby held out her arms.

"It's almost ten o'clock and this little imp has been crying for you for the past ten minutes," Lydia said. "I tried to distract the little darling, but she doesn't want her nanny or me. She wants only her mama to give her her bath."

Right on cue, Caroline babbled what sounded like *mama.*

Tickled that Caroline was beginning to talk, Victoria reached for the baby. "Come here, sweetheart," she said with a wide smile to cover her aching heart. There was nothing better to chase away her unhappiness than holding her baby daughter.

Victoria rubbed noses with the babbling little girl and kissed the tiny hands that pulled at her face and hair. It was true. Whenever it was possible, Caroline's bathing ritual was kept for her, at her request. She looked forward to the moments when she would wash Caroline's soft baby skin, dry her with a warmed towel and rub her tiny body with sweet-smelling baby powder. It was in these moments that she could forget the disturbing moments in the past and allow herself to enjoy the present.

"I'm sorry," she told Lydia with a wry grin. "I'm afraid I was worn-out after May's housewarming party last night."

Victoria hid her face in Caroline's tummy and blew air bubbles. If ever she needed to remember what she could lose if she allowed the past to intrude, these precious moments with the baby were a reminder.

Lydia busied herself with hanging up the dress Victoria had worn last night. "Have you forgotten May invited you to tea this afternoon?"

"No, I haven't." Victoria pulled a lock of her hair out of Caroline's fist and kissed each dimple on each tiny knuckle before she threw back the bedcovers. "In fact, I am particularly eager to speak to my cousin—the sooner the better."

"So?" Lydia peeked out from the closet. "Something *did* happen at the housewarming to upset you?"

"I'm afraid so. Please stay for a few moments, Lydia." She gave Caroline a hairbrush to distract her. "I met a man at May's housewarming last night, Dan O'Hara. You were right. He's the American I met at May's wedding."

Lydia gasped and covered her lips with her fingers. "He recognized you?"

"Maybe. I honestly don't know. I insisted I wasn't the woman he thought he remembered before

I left. I think I managed to discourage him, but I didn't remain long enough to find out.''

Lydia shook her head and took the brush out of Caroline's mouth. "I sensed you were upset when you came home last night, but I never imagined anything like this. What are you going to do now?"

"Do? Nothing," Victoria answered firmly. As if she needed a reminder of who she was today, she glanced at the lace curtains embroidered with the Baronovian coat of arms. The symbols reminded her she was a member of the royal family and had been married to her country's ambassador before she had assumed the post upon his untimely death. "I made a bargain with Rolande and I intend to keep it," she said softly. "I will never do anything to hurt his memory."

Guilt flooded her again. She had to forget Dan. She had to forget the touch of his lips against her throat out on the patio last night and the thrill of having his hand caress her bare back.

Lydia wiped a tear from the corners of her own eyes. "It's my fault for urging you to go to May's housewarming last night!"

"Please don't blame yourself. I knew that once I came to Washington, meeting Dan was bound to happen sooner or later. He is my cousin's husband's best friend, after all. Please, don't worry. I'll be fine."

Lydia didn't look convinced. "Perhaps, but you

are young. I pray no harm comes from this meeting.''

Victoria threw the bedcovers aside, put on her robe and slippers and plucked Caroline out of the bed. ''Time for your bath, sweetness,'' she told the baby. Before she left the bedroom, she glanced back at Lydia. ''Nothing bad is going to happen. I intend to make sure that it doesn't!''

''IF YOU SUSPECTED Dan O'Hara was the man I met in Baronovia how could you have introduced us last night?''

Her cousin, the Duchess Mary Louise of Baronovia, now May Stevens, gasped. ''Oh, Victoria! I never knew who the man was, any more than you did. I just wanted you to have company and to enjoy yourself during the evening. What can I do to make it up to you?''

''Nothing now,'' Victoria replied. ''I'm afraid it's too late. Somehow Dan tied me in with a woman he said he met at your wedding. He asked questions, but I pretended not to know what he was talking about. I only hope I was able to convince Dan I'm not his mystery woman.''

''Is there nothing I can do to help?''

''You can back me up if he comes back to question you.''

''I'm not very good at telling white lies. At least, that's what my Wade tells me. But I promise to try. I hate to see you so unhappy.''

Victoria crumbled the blueberry scone on her plate and studied the tea leaves at the bottom of her cup of cold tea. In spite of her brave words to Lydia, and now to her cousin, she still felt an ache around her heart.

"Happy? What is happiness?" she finally asked. "It's a different thing to different people. As for me, I have never regretted my bargain with Rolande. Besides, nothing good could possibly come of my meeting with this Dan O'Hara."

"Don't mistake me, Vicky," May answered slowly, as if she debated the wisdom of what she was saying. "From the few remarks you've made about your husband, I know the truth about him. I was fond of Rolande, but I am more fond of you," she went on, compassion shining in her eyes. "You may call me a romantic, but I believe in true love, in destiny. A destiny where even unlikely lovers such as Wade and I were fated to meet and marry," she said as a tender smile curved at her lips. "I only feel you are much too young to remain a widow."

Victoria shook her head. "No woman could have asked for a better husband. Besides, I have Caroline." She thought of the bargain she had made with Rolande. "There is no way I wish to meet Dan O'Hara again."

May waved away the servant hovering by the table ready to refill the teapot with hot water. She lowered her voice in an effort not to be overheard. "I am sure Rolande was a good husband to you.

After all, he was a friend of our family for many years. I also happen to know that the love you shared with him, although admirable, is not enough for a lifetime.''

Victoria gasped and glanced around the sunny breakfast room to see if anyone had overheard her cousin's frank remark. "What you are suggesting?"

Her cousin shrugged. "I'm not suggesting anything. I'm merely saying you should not feel guilty about the way you feel about Dan. Since he and Wade work together and are close friends, I'm sure you will meet him often."

When Victoria remained silent, May asked, "Surely you are not afraid of Dan or what he might say if he decides you were the woman he met just before my wedding?"

"No, of course not," Victoria said without conviction. "I'm afraid of myself…my own reaction to meeting him again. I don't want any complications in my life."

"Not for you, perhaps," May agreed. "But how about Dan? You have to remember you're not alone in this."

Victoria dropped her crumpled napkin on the table, and with a sigh rose to pace the floor. After a few moments in deep thought, she turned back to May. "I do remember there were two of us," she whispered. "In fact, I remember that too well. But I would never do anything to hurt Rolande's memory." Even as she spoke, she had to push away the unforgetable sensation of Dan's lips on hers and his hands on her bare back.

May gestured to the large picture window overlooking the nation's capital's buildings. "Out there is my new country, the United States of America. A country both my husband and your Dan O'Hara serve as naval officers. Dan is an American citizen and so is your daughter…there may come a time when Caroline chooses to claim her birthright."

Victoria interrupted with a sound of protest. "He's not my Dan!" she said, even as she thought about the night before her cousin's fairy-tale wedding. There had been a glint in his eyes and laughter on his lips. That smile had attracted her the night they met and that smile, heaven help her, attracted her even as she thought of it now.

"Perhaps not," May said with a wry smile as she rang for the maid, "but I think it's different with Dan. I recall the way he looked for you last night after you left, Vicky. You left him wondering."

Victoria shook her head. "He asked many questions, but I was careful not to give him any answers. Besides, how could he have recognized me a year and a half later? I've changed the color of my hair and it was dark that night."

"Apparently he recognized you anyway." May grinned unabashedly at the blush that came over Victoria's face.

"I'm afraid so." Unable to meet her cousin's eyes, Victoria looked out the window again. Her first thought was that her cousin was right; Caroline was as much an American citizen as she was a citizen of Baronovia. A status that, particularly in these troubled times at home and throughout the world, might one day be valuable.

Her second thought was one of relief that she hadn't told May about the details of the night she and Dan had first met. How she and Dan had slowly and sensuously undressed each other, then lost themselves in each other. She forced her thoughts away from the passionate interlude. Otherwise, she would have wept.

"You must remember your daughter Caroline is her father's child as well as yours," May went on.

"Dan may be a citizen of the United States, but as far as I'm concerned, the only father my daughter has was Rolande."

"One never knows what tomorrow may bring, thank goodness," May laughed. "The least you can do is to see Dan, to get to know him as a friend. You never know, you might need him one day."

"How?" Victoria whispered. "How do you become friends with a man you once loved and lost?"

May threw her arms around Victoria. "I have plans to visit JAG headquarters this afternoon to meet Admiral Crowley, the Judge Advocate General. He was out of town yesterday and missed my housewarming. Why don't you come with me? Dan is a gentleman. Once you see you have nothing to fear from him, perhaps you will think more kindly of him. As a friend, only a friend,'' she hurried to add when she saw a look of panic come over Victoria's face.

''All right,'' Victoria agreed, even as she felt a stab of fear run through her. Last night had been a gamble; did she dare gamble again? ''I'll go with you for Caroline's sake, but I don't intend to become too friendly.''

May laughed and tucked her arm in Victoria's. ''I'm afraid you already have done the worst you could do,'' she said with a teasing smile. ''Take heart, we don't have to remain at JAG too long.''

Obviously happy now that she had convinced Victoria to meet Dan again, May rang for her maid. ''How strange life is. I happily gave up my diplomatic responsibilities at the same time you acquired yours. Trust me, Vicky. All will go well as long as you are here.''

Victoria wasn't so sure. Caroline, after all, had her birth father's warm bright eyes, the color of his hair. It was up to Victoria to keep Dan and Caroline from meeting, if she wanted her daughter's paternity a secret. She refused to think of Dan as Caroline's father.

''Only if you don't speak of Caroline, particularly to Dan.'' Victoria gazed out the window at the Capitol Building where a large flag announced members of the government were back in session. Like it or not, her cousin was right; Caroline was as much an American as she was a Baronovian.

She was reluctant to go with her cousin to visit JAG headquarters, but the thought of seeing Dan there made her senses sizzle. She simply couldn't afford to feel that way, but deep in her heart she knew she had to see Dan at least one more time before she put him out of her heart forever.

JUDGING FROM the excitement going on outside his office, Dan was sure some well-known celebrities were visiting. He glanced through his office windows in time to see the rush to greet his friend and fellow lawyer, Commander Wade Stevens, and his exquisite, petite royal wife. To his surprise, standing slightly off to one side, and regarding the group with a wistful smile, was the last person he thought to see again so soon—Victoria Bernard. He'd learned her married name, all right, but the learning hadn't made him forget her.

His pulse raced. Last night, in her sexy, clinging black cocktail dress, she'd been exotic, intriguing. Even more so with her enigmatic expression. This morning, in her short emerald-green woolen dress and jacket, accentuating the color of her eyes and revealing long, curvy legs, she was breathtaking. To his surprise, she was smiling.

He remembered the sensation of déjà vu hitting him when he'd been introduced to her the other night. With the exception of her blond hair, he'd had a moment when he was almost certain she could be the woman who had haunted him for months after his return from the Stevens wedding.

He remembered the heart-stopping moment when he'd taken her into his arms on the dance floor and realized she had to be his mystery woman. A woman who, when he came too close with his questions, had disappeared into the night.

He hadn't really believed her when she'd said she didn't remember him. He hadn't believed her when she had denied meeting him in the Baronovia palace gardens. She might have forgotten him, but he hadn't forgotten her.

Even while she denied being that woman, he had only needed to take her in his arms to be convinced of her identity.

He'd spent last night wondering if he would ever see her again. He'd even wondered how, if he ever met her again, he could get her to stand still long enough to talk to him. Now that she was on his territory, maybe this was his chance.

He impatiently raked his fingers through his hair. Cornering the lady and getting the truth, the whole truth, out of her wasn't going to be easy. All he wanted was the truth from her own lips, then he would do his best to forget her.

He should have asked for Victoria's last name long ago while he still had a chance of finding her before the whole world got into the act.

Who was Victoria?

What had happened to her husband?

And why, if she was a recent widow, had she responded to his kiss so passionately last night?

He'd been puzzled by the unhappiness in her parting glance last night, and he was puzzled by her now. There was something so vulnerable about her smile, he was half afraid of insisting on the truth.

It had been a blow to his ego to realize that she had gotten married so soon after spending the midnight hours in his arms on that long-ago night. The biggest blow of all was that he had already been half in love with her.

He took a long, pensive look at his reflection on his monitor screen. He was a graduate of the Naval Academy at Annapolis, fifteenth in his class. He'd been cited for bravery for rescuing a fellow classmate from drowning under an overturned sailboat during a sailing exercise. To top it off, he was a damn good lawyer and had spent the last eight years earning his Lieutenant Commander's gold stripes.

So why was he afraid to go out there and corner Victoria?

Forcing a smile, Dan approached the group cautiously. Just as he was a foot away, Admiral Crowley came out of his office and sauntered over to the small group.

"Glad to see you back at work, Commander." He smiled expansively at Wade's royal wife. "Glad to see you too, Mrs. Stevens. Or is it, Your Grace?"

May Stevens dimpled, glanced up at her husband

and threaded her arm through his. "Mrs. Stevens, please."

"Mrs. Stevens it is. Sorry I couldn't make your housewarming."

May held out her free hand. "Then you will have to come to dinner one night soon." Her husband choked off a laugh. "Of course," she added, with an annoyed glance at Wade, "the invitation will have to wait until I have completed my cooking lessons."

"Take all the time you need," Crowley said amiably. He glanced at Victoria and looked to May for an introduction.

"I'm so sorry, Admiral," May said, laughing. "I was so overwhelmed by all the congratulations I'm afraid I forgot my manners. Victoria, this is Admiral Crowley, the Judge Advocate General. Admiral, may I present my cousin Victoria Esterhazy Bernard? Victoria is the widow of the first Baronovian ambassador to the United States, Rolande Bernard. Victoria is now the ambassador in his place."

Dan backed away before anyone could notice him. Damn! His mystery woman, if she really were his missing mystery woman, was not only a cousin to Wade Steven's royal wife, she was the new Baronovian ambassador to the United States.

The new Baronovian Embassy, the State Department, the United States Navy and the Judge Advocate General himself would have his hide if he stuck his neck out and made waves.

He inched back to his office, lost himself in the crowd. No matter how he felt about Victoria, or what she might or might not have been to him a year ago, he was dead meat if he created a national incident. God help him if he so much as allowed himself to become involved. Crowley was still annoyed with him for his involvement in the attempted murder of Secret Service Agent Mike Wheeler's wife, Charlie Norris.

In Charlie's case, it had been a case of her being in the wrong place at the wrong time, then looking to him for legal help.

In Victoria's case, it was only her strained body language, the vulnerable look on her face last night. Sure as hell, something was bothering her. He hoped it wasn't him.

Dan could hardly believe himself for even thinking of helping Victoria. How could he concern himself with her problem, when she'd behaved as if they were strangers?

Except for those kisses he'd managed to initiate, and the dance he had practically forced her into, he thought wryly, he might have been convinced they had never met before. In his book, her passionate response to his out-of-line kiss had been a dead giveaway, whether she was willing to admit it or not.

Maybe it was just as well she'd denied knowing him, he mused as he watched Victoria shaking hands with the admiral and saying goodbye. She was clearly off-limits.

The only woman who would eventually belong to him and him alone, he reminded himself as he thought of his New Year's resolution, was still five years in the future. And then, he thought grimly, only if he had the luck to find someone as beautiful and exciting as this intriguing Victoria Bernard. He had the hollow feeling that nothing else but her double would do.

Dan watched through the office window while May and her cousin surrendered their visitor passes and waved goodbye. Thank God, he thought as he turned on his computer to go back to his research for an impending case, Victoria's unexpected reappearance in his life was only a coincidence of him being in his office when she came to visit. As long as he kept his mind on his case and his nose in his own business, he had nothing to worry about.

Or did he?

A trail of cold fingers ran up and down his spine as he looked up and saw the swinging doors close behind Victoria.

There was definitely unfinished business between himself and this Victoria Bernard.

Chapter Five

Victoria felt a growing sense of unease as she and her cousin were driven in the embassy's limousine to Charlie Wheeler's home in McLean, Virginia. Even May's tourist-guide descriptions of historical monuments they passed on the way couldn't distract her. Maybe, she mused as she fought to ignore the hollow feeling that lately never seemed to leave her, it was caused by the fleeting look of interest that passed over the new chauffeur's face when he heard their destination.

She would have felt a great deal more comfortable if the driver had been Fritz, Lydia's nephew, a man closer to her own age. It was too bad that he was sidelined with a broken leg and bruised arm after an accident. Fritz was not only her chauffeur, he'd been a friendly coconspirator when the walls of the embassy seemed to close in on her.

Stefan, on the other hand, while outwardly cooperative, was an unknown staff member.

She was never really on her own, anyway, she thought as they drove through Columbus Circle and headed west. As a diplomat's wife, and now a diplomat in her own right, her life had been governed by protocol and rules. What difference did it make if Stefan was a stickler for those rules and wanted to know with whom, where and when she wanted to go? Her life, especially over the last few weeks, had not only been turned upside down, it was an open book.

She watched as the chauffeur slid a small black notebook into his breast pocket after making a notation. Why, in heaven's name, did the man feel it necessary to log a harmless social visit?

"Maybe I should turn back," Victoria finally said. "I'm not sure I should be going with you to Charlie Wheeler's."

An enthusiastic newcomer to the United States, May turned her attention away from pointing out the Jefferson Memorial to look at Victoria. "Why not?"

Victoria bit her lip and glanced at the chauffeur. After a moment of reflection, she pushed the button that rolled up the partition between them.

"Before he died, Rolande told me about how you and Charlie were both victims of a crazed Baronovian nationalist. You, two years ago, and your friend Charlie, last year. He also said that both of you narrowly escaped with your lives. It would give someone ideas if the three of us were seen together."

"Like bad-luck pennies?" May laughed at her simile. "That problem is over. I think your husband was a victim of the well-known Baronovian tendency for melodrama, Vicky. If there were some still-unresolved matters between the United States and Baronovia, I am sure I would have known about it. I might have married an American," she added with a wry smile, "but I am still my father's daughter."

Not quite convinced by her royal cousin's logic, Victoria still had to agree. "Rolande was a warrior, but it was his nature. He said it went with his position as ambassador."

May waved away Victoria's concern. "The culprits who were involved then are either awaiting deportation or are in Baronovian prisons. I'm sure nothing bad will happen at the official opening of the embassy, Madame Ambassador. Relax. Try not to worry so much."

Relax! Victoria shuddered. How could she relax when she was confronted with a problem more personal than some possible diplomatic intrigue?

Now that she'd met Dan O'Hara again, after the kiss she and Dan had exchanged at the housewarming, her intuition of impending disaster was stronger than ever. She was torn by the truth; even as she'd feared the outcome of encountering him again, she'd welcomed his kiss. What if she hadn't gotten over him? What would happen the next time they met?

How could she relax when she recalled that even

Lydia had sensed something had disturbed her at the housewarming party?

What would happen if someone guessed Dan was Caroline's father?

"Perhaps you're right," she said reluctantly. "But I can't ignore the feeling that it would be ill-advised for you, Charlie and myself, to be seen together. We could be a target for some terrorists."

"Nonsense. This is a country where a woman is allowed to make her own decisions and to decide for herself who will be her friends," May said firmly. "Besides," she gestured to the window that separated the limousine's driver from the passengers, "your driver is here to protect you."

Protect her? Victoria bit back a comment. She didn't feel safe no matter what her cousin said. May had married an American naval officer and had all the protection he and his country could surround her with. *She* had to depend on her own countrymen for her safety. Worse yet, she had to depend on the very men and women who, according to her late husband, might still be angry at the new diplomatic ties between her country and the United States.

She sat back against the plush leather cushions and tried to take May's advice. "Asserting one's independence might be acceptable here," she finally said, "but not if it might bring about another near-tragedy."

May scoffed at the idea. "Not to worry. We will be safe at Charlie Wheeler's. Did I ever tell you that

Charlie is married to Mike Wheeler, a top United States Secret Service agent? The man has a positive passion for security.''

"No," Victoria answered as another shock wave ran through her. Charlie was the woman who had almost gotten herself kidnapped by the disgruntled head of the old Baronovian Trade Mission. Victoria gazed out the window at the passing landscape and felt more apprehensive than ever.

"Charlie says that as soon as Mike found out she was expecting their first child," May laughed, "he had every alarm system available on the market installed on their property. So you see, you will be protected there, too."

"I'm glad I left Caroline home today." Victoria thought of her baby daughter. Blond and blue-eyed, the baby was the only one in her life to give her unconditional love. "I would never forgive myself if anything happened to frighten her."

"If it will make you feel better, Vicky, we won't stay long today," May said sympathetically. "We can bring the baby another time, if you like. I'm sure Caroline would love to see the animals in Charlie's zoo."

If we come back. Victoria shivered, then chided herself for having foolish fears. "I hope the animals are friendly. Are they in cages?"

May laughed. "I'm sure. Wait until you see Boomer."

"Who is this Boomer?"

"He's Charlie's little pet kangaroo."

Victoria felt herself grow pale. "Kangaroo? Kangaroos are friendly?"

May laughed again. "This one obviously is. I even heard that Boomer was a member of Charlie's wedding party!"

Victoria was wide-eyed at the mental picture of a kangaroo standing at the side of the bride. "A member of the wedding party! Really!"

"Yes, really." May lowered the glass partition and directed the chauffeur to the country road leading to their destination. "Charlie says Boomer has become very attached to her husband."

The look of dismay that came over Victoria's face sent May into gales of laughter. "You will have to get used to the way things operate around Charlie," she said between hiccups. "They might sound odd, but they seem to make sense in an insensible way."

The limousine pulled into the gravel-laced driveway. Amid the crunch of tires on gravel, the front door burst open and a young boy dashed out of the house to meet the car. Behind him, following at a more sedate pace and calling to him to wait up, was a tall, blithe spirit and a very pregnant woman.

"Jake!" she called. "Watch out for the car! You know you're not supposed to be out here alone! Wait up!"

May wrestled with the door handle and slid outside to meet her friend. "That's Charlie and her five-year-old stepson, Jake,'' she laughed over her shoulder. ''Charlie is expecting her first child soon.''

''Congratulations.'' Victoria recalled with envy her pregnancy and the birth of Caroline, the only child she would ever have.

Charlie caught up with her stepson and held him firmly by his shoulders. ''I'm so sorry.'' She kept a firm grip on Jake and put out her other hand. ''I'm Charlie Wheeler,'' she said with a welcoming smile. ''You must be the cousin May has told me about.''

Victoria's qualms at finding herself in the company of both May and Charlie suddenly seemed foolish. Her earlier misgivings about the visit faded in the warmth of Charlie's welcome.

In the background, there was the glow of a newly painted yellow house surrounded by beds of flowering bulbs, marigolds and English daisies. There were graceful white lace curtains at the windows. The property was large, but looked fenced in. If there were any cause for alarm, Victoria thought as she gazed around her, it wasn't visible.

''What a precious little boy,'' Victoria said as she traded smiles with Jake. ''I have a little girl of my own at home. Her name is Caroline. She's only nine months old, but she's very active. I think she's going to be a tomboy when she gets a little older.''

''I've been hoping for a little sister for Jake to play with.'' Charlie aimed a quelling look at a squirming Jake. ''Maybe being a big brother will slow him down.''

"You don't know the baby's sex?"

Charlie shrugged. "In the beginning, Mike and I wanted to be surprised. Now that we've come this far, we've decided to wait until the baby is born." She smiled over Jake's head at Victoria. "I should have welcomed you to the United States, Victoria. I hope your stay in the States will be a happy one."

Victoria blinked, her newfound euphoria vanished and her uneasiness returned at the word *hope*. "Please call me Vicky. And thank you for your welcome," she added wryly, "but you only hope?"

Charlie grinned sheepishly. "I'm sorry. Considering the unfortunate history attached to your embassy, that *was* an unfortunate expression for me to use."

Victoria forced a smile. Charlie hadn't actually used the word, but it appeared her husband hadn't been the only one who thought the new embassy might be jinxed.

"I suppose it's because I suddenly realized that all three of us have or have had some connection with the Baronovian embassy." Charlie glanced at May as if for help. "I'm afraid the last two years have been more than a little exciting, if not downright dangerous."

"All that is behind us now," May said firmly. "With the imprisonment of the men who tried to kill my father and myself, and with the arrest of the man who stalked you, there is no longer a problem."

Victoria shivered. She tried to feel nonchalant

about the embassy's violent history, but it wasn't working.

"Of course." Charlie kept Jake's hand in hers and led the way to the house. "If there's anything brewing, Mike hasn't told me about it. Let's go inside. I'll show you my zoo and you can meet Boomer. He's everyone's favorite."

Victoria remembered the chauffeur who remained waiting by the limousine. From the way his eyes kept darting around checking their surroundings, she began to wonder what was behind his unusual interest. And worse yet, why display such pent-up impatience when a chauffeur's job entailed a great deal of patience?

"In a moment. I have to speak to Stefan. He will want to know when we will be ready to leave."

"There's no hurry, is there?"

"I'm afraid there is," Victoria said. "I have to attend a…what you call…ah, yes, a 'coffee' with a few of my late husband's former colleagues later today."

"Let the man go, Vicky." May pulled out her cell phone. "I'll call Wade and ask him to come for me in an hour. I'm sure he'll be happy to drop you off on the way home."

Victoria was loath to disagree. After sensing there was definitely something strange about Stefan, maybe going home with Wade and May was a good idea. As for thinking of Dan O'Hara, the thought of him was better left in the past where it belonged.

"Stefan—" Victoria joined the chauffeur at the limousine "—you may leave now. My cousin and her husband will take me home."

He straightened. "I'm sorry, madam. My orders are to remain with you at all times."

Victoria stared at him, suddenly feeling as if she were in jail and he was the keeper. "Your orders? From whom?"

"Your chargé d'affaires, madam."

"I'm not aware I needed a bodyguard," Victoria said firmly. "You must be mistaken." She paused for a moment. Maybe the rumors of continued trouble were more real than she'd thought, or her father wouldn't have gone to such lengths to protect her. "Who and what exactly are you?"

Stefan shrugged. "Your chauffeur, madam."

"In that case," Victoria said, "I give you permission to leave. I intend to go home with my cousin." As she spoke, she noticed a grim look come into Stefan's eyes.

Stefan doffed his hat. "Yes, madam."

With a last look in the chauffeur's direction, Victoria headed back to her hostess. To her surprise, young Jake hung back and smiled up at her. "I wish you'd brought your baby so I could play with her."

Victoria was touched. "Caroline is a little young to play with, but I'll try to remember to bring her here when she gets a little older." She squeezed Jake's moist little hand. "I hear you have a zoo in your backyard. Even a live kangaroo."

Jake skipped a couple of steps. "Yep," he said with a disarming grin. "Boomer and I are friends. You'll like him, wait and see."

Victoria grinned back. Obviously, Jake was used to being around pets. She wasn't. The only pet she had ever known up close was Lydia's ancient one-eyed cat. The cat was so lazy she stirred only to eat.

Charlie undid the lock on a gate that stretched across a section of the back end of her property. Instead of going through the gate and inviting everyone to join her, she whistled.

Victoria heard a bark, and before she knew what was happening, a small kangaroo came hopping out from behind a stand of eucalyptus trees. Not just one kangaroo, but two.

To Victoria's dismay, the first kangaroo hopped toward her and cocked its head. She took a step back and grasped Jake's hand more tightly than before. "What does he want?" she whispered, never taking her eyes off the animal.

"He's waiting for a treat," Jake answered. "If you don't have one, all you have to do is hold out your hand with your palm down. He knows that means you didn't bring anything for him. But the next time you come," Jake added in a confidential tone that made Victoria wonder if Boomer understood human speech, "maybe you'd better bring him something." He paused for a moment and eyed Boomer's silent companion. "Guess you'd better bring something for his girlfriend, too."

"Something?"

"Well, I like peanut butter and jelly sandwiches. I think Boomer and his girlfriend Lila do, too."

Victoria cast a cautious eye on Boomer. "Peanut butter and jelly sandwiches?"

Charlie came up alongside them in time to hear Jake's comment. "Boomer doesn't eat anything that walks or talks. Neither will his friend, Lila. I think they must be vegetarians."

Victoria began to think she had somehow wandered into a modern version of Wonderland. And that Alice and the other characters in the book would come popping out of the landscape.

When she heard men's voices coming up the path toward her, she had a sudden feeling that something momentous was going to happen. Maybe she shouldn't have been in such a hurry to dismiss the chauffeur.

Charlie made a megaphone out of her hands and called, "Mike! We're back here!"

Victoria recognized one of the voices as belonging to Wade, May's husband. One was Charlie's husband, Mike. Alarmed, she had the sinking feeling the third voice she heard had to be the voice of Dan O'Hara!

She eyed the three handsome men. One wore a conservative black suit and tie—Mike Wheeler. The other two—Wade and Dan—were dressed in dark blue uniforms with three gold stripes on their sleeves.

As soon as Boomer heard Mike's voice, he barked and bounded down the path to join him. Seconds later, Mike Wheeler came streaking by.

"Hold up, Mike!" Charlie called, choking back the laughter in her voice. "Where are you going?"

"Hold open the damn gate," Mike shouted as he streaked by. "When Boomer follows me inside, I'll double back and you close the gate behind me! For God's sake," he shouted after a quick glance behind him, "do it now!"

Charlie dashed for the wooden gate and held it open. Mike streaked through, dodged a determined Boomer, turned and raced back through the gate. Charlie, between bursts of laughter, locked the gate behind him.

"Thank the Lord," Mike gasped as he bent over, hands on his knees, trying to catch his breath. "Doesn't that fool kangaroo know he's too big to keep jumping on me?"

May, Wade and now Dan were holding their sides laughing. Her heart beating wildly, Victoria welcomed the distraction. Anything to take Dan's avid gaze off her.

"It's been like this ever since Boomer first laid eyes on Mike," Charlie gasped, unable to keep a straight face.

Looking as if he didn't know whether to laugh or curse, Mike finally straightened up. "I told you before and I'm telling you again, Charlie. It's either that kangaroo or me. One of us has got to go!"

Charlie tried to soothe her exhausted husband. "Boomer is only a baby. I'll have a talk with him."

"Baby? Have a talk with him?" Mike eyed his wife under narrowed eyebrows. "The fool doesn't understand English, at least not when I'm doing the talking. Furthermore, the only baby around here has yet to make its appearance. Get used to the idea!"

Charlie patted him on his shoulder. "Come on, honey. I want you to meet someone." She drew him over to Victoria. "Mike, meet Victoria Bernard, the wife of the late Baronovian ambassador to the States. Victoria is the ambassador now. Victoria, this is my cowardly husband, Mike. He's just back in town after being away."

Her husband drew a deep breath and wiped his shaking hands on the jacket of his black suit—the unofficial uniform of the Secret Service. "Don't mind me," he apologized. "I swear I only behave this way around Boomer." He cast a jaundiced glance at his wife. "At any rate, I'm pleased to meet you, Victoria. By the way," he added with a look over his shoulder, "have you met Dan O'Hara?"

Victoria felt her heart plunge to her knees as she thought of May's advice. How could she avoid Dan if everywhere she went people kept introducing them? How could she try to be friendly with him when they were already much more to each other than mere friends?

"I'm pleased to meet you," she said, schooling herself to remain distant and holding out her hand as if they were strangers. Seconds later, when his narrowed eyes met hers, she realized her polite gesture had been a mistake. May and Wade already knew she and Dan had been introduced at their housewarming. May didn't look surprised, but she could see that she'd managed to whet Wade's curiosity.

There could never be just friendship between herself and Dan, she realized as their hands met. Not when the mere touch of his hand on hers managed to create an electric shock that ran up her arm, across her breast and down to her middle.

To add to her dismay, the look in Dan's eyes changed from curiosity to renewed interest. She could almost read his mind—a friendly handshake would never be enough for him. And, heaven help her, she knew it wouldn't be enough for her, either.

Dan held Victoria's hand a moment longer than courtesy called for, but somehow he didn't care. Bystanders were forgotten now that he had another chance to see Victoria again. The woman, he'd finally decided to his pleasure, had to be his mystery woman. It might not come to anything, but at least he had that solution.

"I'm glad to meet you again, too," he answered with an accent on *again,* even though she hadn't used the word. Mystery woman or not, he seemed to care for her—more than was good for him. To add to his dilemma, there was a look in her eyes that told him she cared for him, too. He reluctantly released her hand.

May started back to the house with her husband. "Vicky, you'd better come along if you still want to make that coffee party tonight. Wade and I will drop you off at the embassy."

"...'bye, Vicky," Charlie called to Victoria, as they turned away. "Don't forget to bring your little Caroline with you when you come back!"

Momentarily distracted by Jake Wheeler darting in front of him to reach Victoria, Dan stumbled into her. Instinctively, he reached to keep her from falling.

"Sorry about that," he said, cradling her in his arms before he set her on her feet. He was about to release her when another moment of déjà vu smacked him between his eyes. This was the second time in the last few days he had a chance to hold Victoria. Both times, although she'd denied it, he would have sworn she was the woman he'd held in his arms in Baronovia.

He was debating his next move when he heard Charlie ask if she'd said something amiss. It was then that he looked down at Victoria and realized she was not only shocked, her face had turned white.

Something was wrong.

Chapter Six

Surprised by the sudden silence that had fallen, Dan glanced around him. May stood frozen in place with her fingers held to her lips. Wade and Mike looked uncomfortable. Charlie was still bewildered.

Everyone's reaction to his catching Victoria before she fell definitely wasn't normal.

Dan's suspicions of Victoria's identity resurfaced like an explosion, but from the stunned look on her face, he was damn sure it wasn't a good idea to continue to hold Victoria in his arms.

It might be the wrong time and the wrong place to get some answers, but he wasn't going to give up. Now, he not only had Victoria's identity to prove to his satisfaction, he intended to find out why the mention of "little Caroline" had upset everyone.

Although the chances for a heart-to-heart with Victoria were slim to none, he had plenty of time. In the meantime, for her sake and maybe even his, he'd go along with whatever game she was playing.

He studied Victoria. "Is little Caroline your daughter?" he asked, to the thick tension that filled the air.

"Yes...yes." To his surprise, she glanced at May and hesitated before she answered.

Victoria's terse answer, coupled with the horrified expression on May's face was odd. The hairs stood up on the nape of his neck as he began to sense something was terribly wrong.

Or, was something finally right?

Was Victoria Bernard his mystery woman?

Why had she looked so devastated at the mention of her baby daughter?

She looked as if she wanted to avoid him, and yet, he caught a glimpse of need in her eyes whenever she looked at him. Even now.

The more he thought about the strained situation, the more he became convinced she was trying to hide more than her identity.

Victoria could deny it for a month of Sundays, but every time he'd had her in his arms, she'd turned into the fascinating woman he'd encountered at the Stevens's wedding—except for that blond hair.

As for her having a child, she *was* a widow. So why had she become so upset when Charlie Wheeler had mentioned her daughter, Caroline?

And why, he wondered, had May looked so horrified when Charlie had asked Victoria to bring the baby on her next visit?

To add to Dan's puzzlement, May poked her husband in the ribs. After trading glances with his wife, Wade cleared his throat. "Sorry, I'm afraid we'll have to cut this visit short. I have to get Victoria back to the embassy. Coming, Dan?"

From the set expression on her face, Dan sensed he was the last person Victoria cared to have sitting beside her in a closed car.

There would be time to talk to Victoria later, to find out what about him troubled her. Only not just now. "No, thanks," he said casually, "I think I'll hang around and visit for a while. You go on ahead."

Wade nodded, a short quick nod that mirrored Dan's own consternation at the unexpected finish of a visit that had ended before it began. "Okay. We'll see you guys later."

Troubled, Dan watched the trio disappear around the house. After having been brought here by Wade this afternoon to see Boomer again, he'd naturally expected to leave with him. If anything confirmed something was unusual, if not wrong, it was the abrupt way Wade had agree to leave without him.

Mike cleared his throat. "How about staying for dinner, Dan? Charlie's making roast beef hash, at Jake's request. That, and peanut butter and jelly sandwiches are his favorites. I'll drive you home later."

Dan rubbed his forehead at the sound of tires sliding on the gravel driveway. Though he seemed outwardly calm, every nerve in his body was clamoring for answers. "No, thanks, I'll just call for a taxi. But I sure would like to know what that was all about."

Mike shook his head. "Beats me. Charlie?"

Beside her husband, Charlie was still shaking her head. "I don't know what went wrong. We were just talking about children when Victoria mentioned she had a nine-month-old daughter, Caroline. I'd just asked her to bring the baby with her the next time she comes to visit when you showed up. I still don't know what I said that was wrong."

Dan frowned. "A baby? Why should that upset her?" When Charlie couldn't answer, he stared off in the distance, then finally shrugged. "Maybe. But I'd still like to know why she and May looked as if they'd just seen a ghost when you asked Victoria to bring her baby with her the next time she dropped over."

THAT EVENING Victoria stood gazing down at her daughter lying in her crib. The room was lit by a Mickey Mouse night light and revealed Caroline dressed in a warm bunting, fast asleep with her little rear in the air. Her breath came in little puffs between her pursed lips. A thumb was lodged in the corner of her mouth.

A fierce determination to protect the baby came over Victoria as she gently removed the tiny thumb and tucked the blanket around her. Settling into her new life in the city where Dan worked and lived was difficult enough without worrying that he knew about Caroline.

It was Dan and the threat of his wanting to see Caroline that disturbed her so. Caroline already had a parent who loved her and a bright future as the daughter of a royal Baronovian widow. What would happen to them if Dan eventually guessed the truth? What if he decided to claim his parental rights?

She tried to shake off the feeling of impending disaster. Not even the tiny sighs of contentment Caroline made in her sleep were enough to calm her fears. The immediate problem facing her was the baby's resemblance to her natural father; it was too strong to ignore. It hadn't mattered when they'd been separated by thousands of miles, but it mattered now.

Would she be the only one who noticed the resemblance between Dan and Caroline? Was she the only one who would notice their killer smiles and the clefts they both had in their chins?

What would people think if, God forbid, they saw Dan and Caroline together?

She swung around at a slight sound at the nursery door. Lydia stood in the doorway dressed for bed in her robe and slippers.

"After I saw you at dinner, I knew I would find you here." Lydia came into the room and gently closed the door behind her. "What happened this afternoon to disturb you so, my dear?"

Victoria averted her eyes and gazed down at her

daughter. Not even for Lydia and the confidences they'd shared could she bring herself to reveal her fears for her daughter's future in case Dan wanted to reveal that he was Caroline's natural father. And, heaven help her, the surprising depth of her physical response to Dan this afternoon. "How do you know something happened?"

"I know you too well." Lydia closed the door behind her and joined Victoria at the side of the crib. She glanced down at the sleeping baby. "You can't be worried about Caroline, she looks as peaceful as an angel. It's you I worry about. You looked so upset at dinner tonight."

Victoria smiled wanly and wrapped her arms around herself as if seeking a comfort that wasn't there.

Lydia smiled her sympathy. "You're too good an actress to have given yourself away to just anyone. To someone who knows you as well as I do, that's another story. Your eyes gave you away."

The door to the adjoining bedroom, already half-opened, opened all the way. Caroline's nanny peeked around the door. "Is something wrong, madam?"

Victoria shook her head. "No, I just wanted to say goodnight to Caroline. Go back to sleep. I'm sorry I disturbed you."

Victoria took a long, loving look at her daughter and with a finger at her lips, led Lydia out of the nursery.

"I met Dan O'Hara again this afternoon," she confessed. "You know, the man I met back home and again at May's party," she began as soon as she led Lydia to her own bedroom. "May and I were visiting a friend of hers when he unexpectedly showed up and her friend told me to bring the baby with me the next time I visited. Charlie, May's friend, didn't know that Dan didn't know about Caroline."

"And he does now?"

"I'm afraid so, now that May's friend gave it away. At least, he knows I have a daughter, but that's all." Distraught, Victoria paced the floor of her bedroom, picking up and dropping pieces of clothing. "So far he'd only suspected I was the woman he encountered at May's wedding. After today, it looks as if he's becoming more and more convinced. It's only a matter of time before he puts one and one together and gets the right answer."

"Ah." Lydia's voice was thoughtful. "Have you ever regretted giving yourself to him that night?"

"No," Victoria said fiercely. "If I hadn't met Dan, I wouldn't have had Caroline. But that's not what seems to nag at him. He wants to know if I was that woman. I thought I'd forgotten all about him," she said, "but the truth is I fell in love with him that night, and, to my guilt, I love him still. Nothing can come of it, but I worry what he might do if he ever sees Caroline."

"He can't possibly know he's her father—unless

you tell him," Lydia said reassuringly. "Even if he knows Caroline is his child, I'm sure he won't tell anyone. If he's part of the United States military, he must be a gentleman. You have nothing to worry about."

"I wish," Victoria answered as she recalled the questioning look in Dan's eyes this afternoon. "He doesn't seem to be the kind of man who gives up easily."

"Then he's met his match in you," Lydia said with a wry laugh. "You were the kind of child who listened quietly then did whatever you were determined to do. I remember you drove your mother to distraction more than once. In fact, I'm surprised you allowed your father to marry you off to Rolande without a protest."

"Largely, it was because of family tradition," Victoria answered, her heart aching at the feeling of loss she still remembered. "And because after Dan went home without looking for me, it was too late."

"There's no reason to break your heart over him at this late date," Lydia announced. "Be polite if you meet him again, my dear, and try to put the past behind you."

"That's the problem. I can't forget him." Victoria picked up a small framed photograph of the baby. "I see him every time I look at Caroline. Maybe I'm the only one to see it, but she looks so much like him."

Lydia put an arm around Victoria. "There's no

use worrying about it tonight. Why don't you come down to the kitchen with me? I think we could both use a cup of hot chamomile tea—it might help you to get a good night's sleep.''

"Sleep? I haven't been able to sleep well since I met Dan again at the housewarming last night,'' Victoria said, bone-weary with worry over what Dan might do. "I don't think I'll be able to sleep peacefully again as long as we're here in Washington.''

"With little Caroline to remind you of the man, I know it must be hard to ignore him.'' Lydia filled the aluminum kettle and put it on to boil. "But if he no longer means that much to you, you must try to put him out of your mind.''

"I wish I could,'' Victoria confessed to the woman she'd known all her life, a woman who had been more to her than her own mother. "When I think of Dan, I feel like a woman,'' she went on ruefully. "I can't help remembering that night—it was so wonderful.'' She felt a guilty flush cover her body as she spoke. "I loved my husband, but...''

"...he never made you feel a whole woman. I know.'' Lydia finished the sentence for her. "I am so sorry, love. I have my own memories to keep me warm at night,'' she said quietly. "I think the biggest problem is that you're too young never to have known the intimacies of a real marriage.''

Victoria blushed again at the memory of the night when Dan had wrapped himself around her, caressed her until she was mindless. He'd made her a woman that night and showed her a side of herself she hadn't suspected she had. The pain of having to deny what her body still craved and that her mind warned against seemed almost too much for her to bear.

Lydia busied herself pouring boiling water over tea leaves in a pot and set it aside to steep. She sliced a lemon, reached into the gigantic refrigerator for cream and set them on the table. "I'm sure everything will come out all right in the end, love. Don't let this meeting break your heart again."

"I can't," Victoria said with a catch in her voice and dropped into a chair. "I made a bargain when I married Rolande and I intend to keep it. For Caroline's sake as well as mine. He was a good husband and a loving father—his memory deserves my respect and my loyalty."

"And this man, Dan O'Hara? Do you think you will be able to avoid him?"

"I don't think so," Victoria sighed, distracted at the thought that Dan was her cousin's friend and that their next meeting might not be of her choosing. "I'm sure I'll run into him again sooner or later. Oddly enough, May even suggested I try to become friends with Dan for Caroline's sake."

"For Caroline's sake?" Lydia paused and frowned. "Why for the baby's sake? What does the baby have to do with your being friendly to this man?"

"She said it was in case I might someday need

him and his American citizenship to protect Caroline.'' Victoria shuddered at the thought her baby daughter might need anyone else's protection in addition to her own.

Lydia nodded solemnly as she poured two cups of strong tea. ''God grant that you never will have to.''

IT WAS the night of the new Baronovia Embassy's reception for Washington's diplomatic corps. The first official affair since the embassy had opened. Two floors below the embassy living quarters, florists were placing floral creations around the rooms. Caterers were putting the finishing touches on trays of hors d'oeuvres and tiny meat pastries. Trays of exotic dried fruit and honeyed pastries had been prepared for the Mideastern guests. A fountain of fruit punch had been set up in a corner for those guests who didn't drink liquor.

''You look lovely tonight, as always, my dear.'' Lydia entered the bedroom after a polite knock. ''That shade of blue goes well with your new hair color.''

Victoria started at the sound of Lydia's voice. ''Thank you,'' she said, turning away from the floor-length mirror where she had been lost thinking about Dan O'Hara.

''I'm afraid I haven't been able to reach the zipper at the back of my gown,'' she said with a rueful smile as Lydia came toward her. The truth was that she'd been desperately trying to forget the depth of her sensual longings that were tormenting her to have zipped the dress for herself.

Lydia laughed. "You'd think you would be able to do it properly after all these years of dressing yourself."

Grateful for the distraction from her thoughts, Victoria smiled at her friend and confidante. She could only guess that Lydia was trying to find a way to speak to her privately without appearing to do so. "Only if you help me with this zipper."

"Of course." Lydia came up behind her and gently pulled up the zipper. "You have appeared disturbed lately, my dear. Has something disturbed you?"

Victoria held her breath. She'd tried so hard to hide the uneasy sensation that lingered in her mind like a dark cloud, but Lydia seemed to know her better than she knew herself. "No. What makes you think so?"

"You haven't been yourself lately, my dear. You hardly spoke tonight at supper."

She gazed at Lydia wordlessly. How much of the truth about the way she'd felt after meeting Dan again could she tell her without giving herself away? "Just nerves, I guess. I'm afraid these formal affairs take some getting used to."

"You did well as an ambassador's wife in London," Lydia reminded her, but Victoria could tell from the concern in her eyes that she hadn't convinced her. ''I'm sure you will do well again tonight,'' she went on.

The warmth of Lydia's reassuring hands on her shoulders only managed to bring back flashes of her thoughts the night Dan had caressed her bare back at May's housewarming.

Her late husband's platonic touch, while welcome, hadn't been the same as Dan's. Rolande's touch hadn't created the streaks of electric shocks that had run through her when Dan had caressed her. It didn't awaken the sensuality she'd kept buried within herself since her marriage. Instead, the warmth of Rolande's arms around her served to remind her that he had been her safe haven. She had to be content with that.

Victoria sighed. Why couldn't she have loved her husband as he had deserved to be loved?

She finally pulled away. ''Nothing I can't handle,'' she said, ''but thank you.''

Her father, the embassy's chargé d'affaires assisting her in her new role, appeared in the doorway. He regarded her for a long moment, then, with a look, dismissed Lydia.

''Daughter,'' he began, with an enigmatic look in his eyes. ''You may hear some rumors tonight that could disturb you. Try to remember they are only rumors. But if you become too concerned, don't hesitate to come to me.''

''Rumors?''

''Our security operators have intercepted several

e-mails this morning threatening to disrupt our celebration tonight. We have consulted with the United States State Department and they corroborate that undercurrents of unrest in Baronovia do still exist.''

Victoria remembered the stories her late husband had told her of earlier demonstrations and even shootings. ''You mean that there might be trouble tonight?''

''It means that there are still some people that are disturbed about our alliance with the United States.'' He shrugged, but Victoria knew the situation was serious or he wouldn't have warned her.

''I understand. I'll be careful,'' Victoria said. She reached for the satin handbag that matched her dress and smiled bravely at her father. ''I'm ready.''

In spite of her outwardly cheerful manner, a wave of fear passed over Victoria as she recalled the stories of the earlier demonstrations and attempted the kidnapping of her cousin May almost two years ago. Did her father think she might be the next target of some crazed nationalist?

''Papa, please wait a moment,'' she said. ''I thought the agreements between the two countries were signed long ago.''

''They were. Unhappily, there seems to be a new wave of unrest throughout our country. Don't be alarmed, my dear, just be careful,'' he went on as he took her arm. ''Until matters have been resolved to our mutual satisfaction, the United States Treasury Department has graciously agreed to help us in this matter.''

''Help us? How?'' Rather than finding his information reassuring, her fears grew with every passing moment.

''The Treasury Department has assigned several Secret Service Agents to work with our people to guard you and Caroline.''

''My God…Caroline!'' Victoria started for the bedroom door. ''I have to see her and make sure she's safe!''

''Wait a moment, my dear.'' Her father put his arm around her and held her close to him until her heartbeat returned to normal. ''I've already spoken to Caroline's nanny and to Lydia about the importance of not leaving the baby alone. They have both promised to guard her with their lives tonight.''

Chapter Seven

With her father's words of reassurance ringing in her ears, Victoria followed him to the elevator. The silence between them, broken only by the deep hum of the elevator as it slowly descended the two floors to the ballroom below, felt ominous.

With the family living quarters two floors above the ballroom, how could she hear anything going on upstairs? Knowing that the United States Secret Service would be on hand tonight didn't help. She wasn't afraid for herself; her fears were for her daughter.

A shudder ran through her as she thought of the long night still ahead of her. There would be at least a hundred guests in attendance, most of whom she'd never met before. Was it possible the person who had sent the threatening e-mail would be amongst them?

Her father glanced at the tormented look on her face and took her cold hand in his. "Don't worry, my dear. Everything will be fine tonight. I only asked for additional protection to play it safe. You know that you and Caroline mean the world to me.''

"Yes, I know. Thank you," she murmured, then caught a glimpse of the somber look that came over her father's face at her reply. Her spirits dropped even further when she realized she'd spoken to him as though they were polite strangers, instead of a father and daughter discussing life-threatening matters.

When had her attitude toward her father begun to change? Victoria wondered. When had she gone from being grateful for her father consenting to come to the United States to help her to a strong woman who could manage for herself? Did her father realize how much she'd changed?

"Papa, wait a moment." She caught her father's arm as the elevator doors slid open. There was no way she could let him go on thinking he had to take care of her. Especially on a night so special. He had to know how much she cared about him, even though she'd grown up and away from him. "You forgot a kiss for good luck."

"Of course." Her father smiled and bent to kiss her lightly on her forehead. When their eyes met, Victoria saw a new respect for her in his eyes.

She glanced at her watch; it was eight o'clock. With the celebration about to begin, the frantic activity going on around them ended abruptly. Florists and caterers disappeared behind closed doors, servers in livery straightened to attention. The embassy's social secretary was indicating the receiving line. Glancing at the front door, she noticed the chauffeur, Stefan. She was about to inquire why when her father followed her gaze.

"Something wrong, my dear?"

"No," she answered and forced a smile. She might be surprised by Stefan's presence, but this was no time to question it. Tonight was the time to celebrate Baronovia's arrival into the twenty-first-century world of diplomacy.

"Come then, my dear," her father answered, holding out his arm. "Your cousin, the Duchess Mary Louise, and her husband, Wade, have arrived. They have graciously agreed to help receive our guests tonight."

Victoria took her place in the receiving line. Surely, she thought as she exchanged a smile with May, there would be time later to sort out her troubled thoughts. Surely May, a woman married to the man she loved, would understand.

Victoria caught a glimpse of Mike Wheeler casually mingling with guests. Dressed in a traditional tuxedo and holding a flute of champagne in his hand, he was trying to look as if he were part of the landscape. Instead of being reassured, she felt a premonition that something was destined to happen tonight.

She'd believed in destiny only two times prior to tonight, she thought as she smiled and welcomed another guest. The first time had been the night when Dan O'Hara had claimed her. The second time had been when she had unexpectedly encountered him at May's housewarming. The third could be tonight.

Deep in her own thoughts, she had difficulty remembering the names of the dignitaries being presented to her. The longer the evening went on, the more she felt she was drowning in a sea of unfamiliar faces and unable to swim to shore.

To Victoria's relief, two hours later her father signaled that the members of the receiving line were free to join the other guests. Her mouth was dry from forcing herself to indulge in small talk, her feet, unaccustomed to her new sapphire satin slippers, ached. With the excuse that she needed to go upstairs and change her shoes, she started toward the elevators.

Before she had a chance to make her exit, she saw a late guest stride in and murmur to the embassy's social secretary. Dan O'Hara!

She watched with a sinking feeling while the social secretary, his eyebrows raised at the evident lack of a written invitation, motioned Dan in.

It only took Dan a moment to locate the woman he'd come here to talk to. First he had to thank May and Wade Stevens for his invitation.

May, royal duchess that she was, greeted him politely. From the wary look in her eyes, Dan sensed May had been very reluctant to extend tonight's invitation. She'd only agreed after he'd begged for a chance to make his peace with Victoria. May's husband, Wade, shook Dan's hand.

"Now that we've gotten you in here, for Pete's sakes," Wade muttered under his breath, "try to stay out of trouble. If Victoria won't talk to you, let it go."

"I swear," Dan solemnly said and slowly moved on to where Victoria seemed frozen in place. To his distress, the expression on her face was fear—the same expression he saw there every time he encountered her.

Tonight she wore a sapphire-blue gown that complemented the color of her eyes. Long diamond earrings dangled from her ears and lit up her face. Her neck was bare. If ever there was a case of less is more, Victoria's lack of adornment was it. He bit back a surge of desire, the need to take her in his arms.

Dan felt as if a dam was about to burst inside him. Pent-up desire raced through him as Victoria met his eyes. Mystery woman or not, Victoria was the most beautiful and desirable woman he'd ever met.

But she made it clear she could never be his.

He was filled with regret. The most he could hope for was that she would eventually come to trust him instead of looking like a frightened deer caught in a car's headlights whenever they met. Someday, he promised himself, he would find out what there was about him that frightened her so.

When he finally approached Victoria, he forced a smile. "Mrs. Bernard—er…Victoria?"

Victoria forced herself to focus on Dan. Tonight, instead of his blue uniform, he was dressed in a black tuxedo, complete with starched white shirt and onyx studs. The cleft in his chin drew her gaze like a magnet. It was identical to the little dimple in Caroline's chin. Her heart began to beat rapidly. In or out of uniform, Dan O'Hara was man enough and handsome enough to break her heart.

"How did you get here?" she asked.

Dan flushed at the blunt question. He ran his fingers around his neck; the bow tie suddenly seemed too tight. "No need to worry," he said with a rueful smile. "I was invited."

Victoria frowned. How could she have been so distracted by her thoughts of Dan that she hadn't noticed his name on the guest list? She shook her head. "If you had been on the guest list, I'm sure I would have noticed."

"What would you say if I told you your cousin invited me?"

Victoria gazed at him quietly, but he sensed the tension in her. "I'd say you were either making up a story or taking advantage of May's position and her husband's friendship."

Dan held up his right hand. "I swear it's the truth. I have to admit I asked May to invite me. She wasn't keen on the idea, but she graciously agreed after I told her why I had to come here tonight.''

''The Duchess has the right to invite anyone she wants to the grand opening of her country's embassy,'' Victoria replied. ''But that doesn't answer my question. *What* are you doing here?''

''I came to apologize,'' Dan said somberly. In his heart, he knew it had been more than an apology that had brought him here tonight. He'd had to see Victoria one more time. Not only because she was an intriguing puzzle, but because, day or night, she continued to haunt him. He was sure she was his mystery woman, but he had to find out what bothered her whenever they met. Once that problem was settled, he'd told himself, he'd get out of her life for good.

The problem was that he wanted her now in the same way he'd wanted her that night in the palace gardens. He wanted her, even though he knew she was lost to him.

''Apologize? For what? And why tonight?'' She looked ready to run away again, but at least she was listening to him. To his way of thinking, a good sign.

''In answer to your first question,'' he said, ''I'm here to apologize for whatever I may have said or done the other day to disturb you. As for your second question, I thought you'd be more inclined to listen to me if you had May and Wade nearby to protect you.''

Again, wariness flickered through her eyes. How much did he know about the recent e-mail threats? "Protect me from what?"

Dan felt like a dog. Considering the rumors of unrest he'd heard recently that involved the embassy, *protect* was an unfortunate choice of words. All he'd accomplished was to frighten her.

"Not from what, from me," he said wryly. "Every time we happen to bump into each other, you run. I never seem to be able to finish a conversation with you."

"In the first place," Victoria answered after a moment's pause, "since you've obviously made a mistake about knowing me, there is nothing to forgive. As for my allowing you to remain here tonight, you are May's guest, not mine. As I said before, my cousin has the right to invite anyone she wishes to attend this affair."

Dan thought of the Shakespearian quote, "...the lady doth protest too much, methinks." There *was* something about him that bothered her. He'd been a lawyer long enough to see through that look in a guilty person's eyes. She might insist they were virtual strangers, but her eyes said something else. He wouldn't have been all that surprised to learn she was just as attracted to him as he was to her.

He smiled at her. "Has anyone ever told you your eyes give you away?"

Victoria blushed at the intimate question. It was true. From the time she'd been a small child, she'd never been able to hide what she was thinking. Her father had even said her thoughts were engraved on her forehead. Even Lydia had told her the look in her eyes gave her away.

Dan not only knew her better than she'd thought he did, he seemed determined to have her share those thoughts with him! Alarm signals sounded at the back of her mind. It was time to break off the conversation before she managed somehow to reveal what she felt honor-bound to conceal.

"If you don't mind, I have to leave you now," she said politely. "I'm sure my cousin and her husband will be happy to entertain you. That is, if you choose to stay."

Choose to stay? Dan watched Victoria stop to speak to an embassy staff person and then disappear into the elevator. He had intended to stay as long as there was a chance he could talk to her, and nothing had changed his mind.

Damn! he thought as he made his way around the room to the bar. Maybe his coming here tonight hadn't been such a good idea, after all.

The door to the library was open when he finally reached the hall that separated the ballroom from the rest of the building. Attracted by the wall of books, he glanced around to make sure no one was in there and sauntered inside.

In addition to the books, many of them with foreign titles, there was a magnificent hand-carved desk. Maybe, he thought with a bow to his conscience, he could at least leave Victoria a note. He'd tell her he had finally decided she wasn't the woman he remembered meeting in Baronovia and that he wished her well.

He'd even ask Mike Wheeler to deliver the note before he called it a night.

The desk was covered with family photographs. One small photograph was of the late ambassador, his wife Victoria and their baby daughter.

A wave of nostalgia hit him as, with a pang of envy, he recalled his own parents—or rather, his lack of parents. Orphaned at an early age, he'd been adopted by his elderly uncle, a former naval officer. Patrick O'Hara had nurtured him through adolescence before he'd firmly set him on the road to Annapolis. Fortunately for him, and unfortunately for his uncle, he'd chosen law school and the Judge Advocate General Corps instead of opting for the submarine service his uncle was so proud of.

Hoping no one would notice him, Dan dropped into a chair behind the desk and, with a quick glance to reassure himself he was alone, rummaged through the center drawer for paper and a pen. He was idly admiring the Bernard family portrait when he stopped. In the photograph, Victoria had blue-green eyes and long, auburn hair. Her husband had black hair graying at the temples and smoky gray eyes.

The baby in the photograph, on the other hand, had blond hair and blue eyes.

He picked up the framed portrait to look at it more

closely. He was tracing the cleft in the baby's chin when an incredible thought raced through his mind. The baby in the picture not only didn't resemble either of her parents, the longer he looked at her, the more she began to look like a little mirror image of himself as a child!

He set the small, framed picture back on the desk, drew out his wallet and took out his most prized possession: a snapshot of himself as a small child held in his late mother's arms while his father looked down at him. He held the small snapshot against the family portrait and studied it so intently his eyes began to sting.

He'd always been good at math, he told himself, to account for his instinctive reaction. He counted up the months since he and his mystery woman had made passionate love. Judging from the possible age of the baby, even if Victoria had married right away, there was only one possible answer to the question that puzzled him.

Not only was Victoria the woman he'd made love to that long-ago night in the palace gardens, she had borne a child as a result of that encounter! And, unless he was dead wrong in his calculations, the child in the Bernard family portrait was his!

Victoria was afraid of him because he was her child's natural father!

He sank back in the chair and felt as if he'd been kicked in the gut. Not only could he be the baby's natural father, it was damn certain now that Victoria was his mystery lady. That was why she became so distressed every time she looked at him. She was afraid he would discover the truth.

Now, how to convince Victoria to come out from behind the wall she'd thrown around herself and let him in? He was honorable enough to leave the status quo, damn it. He only wanted to know the truth.

To his growing dismay, insisting on the truth might cause another international incident!

There was so much at stake that the enormity of what he wanted to do boggled his mind. He wasn't a lawyer for nothing, he told himself as he gave up the idea of leaving Victoria a note. He crumpled the note of apology he'd started to write. He would gather up all the facts he could get his hands on, then present them to Victoria. She had to listen.

Most of all, he had to find a way not to destroy her reputation.

He had to talk things over with his uncle Pat. Chances were his uncle was in a position to be more objective than he was about the baby and could pass on some helpful advice on how to approach the problem.

He had the truth on his side. All he needed was time.

As he started out of the library, Mike Wheeler entered. "I thought I saw you come in here," he said, glancing at the floor by Dan's feet. "Mind telling me what you're doing?"

Dan followed Mike's eyes. The man was gazing

at the crumpled piece of paper that Dan, in a hurry
to leave, had dropped on the floor. He bent to pick
it up. "I was writing a note for you to give to Victoria."

Mike raised his eyebrows. "I saw you speaking
to the lady a few moments ago. Why would you
want to write her a note now?"

"You wouldn't believe me if I told you."

"Try me."

From the grim expression on Mike's face, Dan
knew this was no ordinary question. Mike knew
him, for God's sakes. He even owed him for helping
to rescue his wife Charlie from the local law, yet
here he was treating him like a stranger—like a suspect!

Something was wrong, he thought as he took in
Mike's official stance, and it wasn't only Dan's
foray into the library.

"I tried to convince Victoria to accept my apology for showing up here tonight," he said, realizing
he sounded like a fool. "That is, I tried to, but she
wouldn't listen."

"Apology not accepted?"

"No. That was why I was writing her a note."

Wheeler glanced at the wad of paper Dan had
picked up and held in his hand. "Something
changed your mind?"

Damn! The man, famous for his caution, was living up to his reputation of being a hard-nosed, se-

curity-conscious man. That they had been friends until a minute ago didn't seem to matter now.

"I was just about to leave and check on an idea I came up with before I tried to speak to Victoria again. Satisfied?"

Mike studied him carefully; long enough to make Dan squirm. "For now," Wheeler said with a pointed look at the door. "You were about to leave?"

"For now," Dan echoed. "But I'll be back."

Mike shrugged. "Just don't make it too soon, there's trouble enough around here without you."

Dan fought his instinctive reaction. It not only sounded as if he was being asked to leave for his own good, he didn't like Mike's attitude. "What kind of trouble?"

Wheeler gazed at him thoughtfully, then glanced around the library as to make sure they were alone. "It's not for publication, but there have been a few threats against the embassy."

"Hell, even I've heard that. What else is new?"

"The threats were largely aimed at Victoria and her daughter. Considering how trigger-happy these Baronovian nationalists appear to be, I'd hate to see you get in the way of a bullet."

"You've got to be kidding!" Dan couldn't believe that history might be repeating itself tonight. "I thought that was all settled when Wade saved his duchess from a kidnapping!"

"Yeah, well, it seems that it wasn't." Wheeler

cracked a rueful smile. "Not even after the second shooting when some jerk tried to kill my wife. Good thing the fool didn't know how to shoot straight."

"And now Victoria? Why?"

Mike grimaced. "Probably because she was married to the late ambassador and had his child. The only good thing to come out of all this malarkey is that Wade married his duchess after he saved her. And that I married Charlie after she managed to save me. If the pattern holds true, Victoria is the next target."

Dan tried to put his warring emotions aside without giving himself away. No way in hell was anyone going to protect Victoria and Caroline without him being involved.

Now all he had to do was to find a way to do it without stepping on anyone's toes.

"Do me a favor, will you?" he asked Mike. "Don't tell anyone you found me in here. And keep an eye on Victoria and her daughter for me."

"What do you mean, keep an eye on Victoria and Caroline *for you?*" Wheeler's eyebrows rose in a V. "What do you have to do with this nationalist baloney?"

"Just what I said," Dan replied, rapidly counting the length of time it would take him to get to his uncle Pat's apartment, run his suspicions about the baby through him and get back to the embassy before tonight's celebration was over. "Keep an eye on them for me. I'll be back."

He could feel Wheeler's eyes on his back as he left, but he didn't care. He'd made up his mind to watch over Victoria and the baby, and that's what he intended to do.

It was a good thing Wheeler hadn't noticed he'd taken the Bernard family photograph and hidden it beneath his tuxedo jacket.

Chapter Eight

Patrick O'Hara, wearing flannel pajamas, a baseball bat at the ready in his hand, frowned at his visitor. He pointed to the grandfather clock in the hallway of his Georgetown condominium as it chimed eleven. "Do you have any idea of the time, me boy?"

Dan grinned. The twinkle in his uncle's eyes gave him away; the old man was glad to see him. The only reason the man had been in bed was for the lack of someone to needle.

His uncle had been his father, mentor and friend ever since Dan had been orphaned. If Pat hadn't resorted to his vast vocabulary of cuss words he'd acquired during his years in the navy's submarine service, things weren't as bad he made them sound.

"Sorry, I couldn't wait until morning." Dan plucked the small color photograph of the Bernard family out of his jacket. "Take a look at this, please."

"As long as you're here, you might as well come in," his uncle growled. He took the photograph and led the way into his den.

Dan dropped onto a leather couch and surveyed the room that had, for many years, been his haven. Photographs of himself at every stage of his life filled one wall, his athletic trophies another. To Dan's chagrin, even some of his better school report cards were on display.

"Who are these people?" His uncle looked up from studying the photograph and finally broke the silence. "Am I supposed to know them?"

"Hang on a minute." Dan went over to the wall and took down a photograph of himself and his late parents, taken when he'd been six months old. He handed over the photograph. "Now compare this photograph with that one. Would you agree there's a strong resemblance between the children?"

His uncle studied both photographs. "They look enough alike to be the same child," he murmured. "But then," he added with a calculating look at Dan, "all babies look alike to this old bachelor. Unless…" He peered into Dan's eyes. "Are you really asking me for my opinion or do you already know the answer?"

"I think so," Dan said. "What would you say if I told you the little girl in the photograph is Caroline Bernard, and her parents the late Baronovian ambassador Rolande Bernard and his wife, Victoria?"

"She looks enough like you to be related by

blood to the O'Haras,'' his uncle murmured as he studied the photograph again. ''Blond hair, blue eyes and that dimple in her chin... Maybe the resemblance is only a coincidence?''

''No coincidence,'' Dan returned. ''Not as far as I'm concerned.'' He dropped back into his chair with a sigh. ''I'm going to tell you a story. I'm not exactly proud of my part in it, so promise me you won't blow up until you hear me out.''

Pat O'Hara, no dummy, gazed at his nephew for a long moment. ''Are you going to tell me you think this child is yours?''

Dan met his uncle's frank gaze and slowly voiced his thoughts. ''Is Caroline mine? The idea of suddenly finding someone who is a part of myself seems improbable, but I've never been so sure of anything in my life.''

His uncle handed back the photographs and sank back into his upholstered armchair. ''Does anyone else think she is your daughter?''

''Her mother, although she has yet to admit it to me. In fact, she acts as if she's afraid of me whenever we meet.'' Dan glanced over at the small bar set up in one end of the den. ''Before I tell you the story behind the photograph, I think something strong to drink is in order.''

His uncle winked. ''Not too strong, my boy. If this is going to be as heavy a story as I think it is, I need my wits about me. Go on to the kitchen and bring me a Guinness. That is, if that housekeeper of mine hasn't made away with it all."

The feistier his uncle became, the more Dan realized the man *was* more deeply touched by the photograph than he cared to admit. Rose Garrett, his housekeeper, a sturdy example of all that went into a good Irish woman, as she continually reminded everyone, had never imbibed anything stronger than tea as long as he'd known her.

He smiled at his uncle's attempt to cover his emotions and headed for the kitchen.

"Here you go." Dan handed a can of beer to his uncle, popped open a can for himself and dropped back into the easy chair.

After Dan took a deep swallow of the tangy brew to fortify himself, he told his uncle how he'd gone to Baronovia to act as the best man at his friend Commander Wade Stevens's wedding over a year ago. He went on to tell him about the magical encounter with his mystery woman. "I'm not the kind of guy for one-night stands, Uncle Pat. I swear I tried to find her the next morning, only it looked as if she didn't want to be found."

"More than a passing fancy, was she?"

"Much more," Dan agreed, surprised to realized that somewhere along the line he'd actually begun to fall in love with Victoria. "Although, to be honest with you, I didn't realize it at the time. I do now. The truth is, I'd never been so taken by a woman before."

"And the lady?"

"As I said, I never saw Victoria Bernard again. That is, not until I met her at a party here in Washington a few weeks ago." Dan took another swallow of beer and thought about the heart-stopping moment when he'd been introduced to Victoria at the Stevens's housewarming party.

"It turns out she's the widow of the Baronovian ambassador to the States," he went on. "To make matters even more touchy, she's also a distant cousin to European royalty."

"Hold on a bit, my boy!" His concern obvious, Patrick held up a hand to stop Dan. "Forget the lady's cousins. It sounds as if they have no part in this. Are you saying this Victoria Bernard wasn't married at the time you met her?"

Dan felt himself flush. "No, she wasn't." He couldn't bring himself to tell his uncle that Victoria had been a virgin at the time of their midnight encounter. And that the timing between that night, Victoria's subsequent marriage and the birth of her daughter strongly suggested Dan could be the father of her child.

His uncle raised an eyebrow and glanced at the photograph again. "From the way you tell the story, it's more than likely the lady didn't give you this photograph to take with you?"

"No, you might say I borrowed it." Dan ignored the disapproval that came over his elderly uncle's face. His uncle may have been a seagoing man, but he was old-fashioned when it came to women. "The point is, I didn't meet her again until the last few weeks. Three times, if you count tonight. And each we meet, dammit," he said as he ran his fingers through his hair, "she acts as if she's terrified to see me!"

Dan rose to pace the den, his footsteps clicking in military cadence as he walked back and forth across the wooden floor. "I *have* to know what there is about me that sets her off whenever she sees me, Uncle Pat. It has to be more than that encounter long ago. Hell, we were two consenting adults back in Baronovia. There has to be a reason why we can't at least talk to each other like two civilized people. Unless…"

"…unless she doesn't want anyone, including her family, to know about you and that night in… What's the name of that place?"

"Baronovia. It's a small mid-European country you've probably never heard of. Neither had I until Wade met his duchess and married her. It's still so old-fashioned and filled with early-twentieth-century customs, I call it a country time forgot."

"Seems to me that's all the more reason the lady doesn't want to have the truth about your er…your encounter to come out. She wasn't raised to behave the way she did with you. Especially if the child is yours."

"I think it's more than that. I only wish…" Dan began, then he shrugged helplessly. "To tell you the truth, I'm not even sure I know what I wish for anymore.''

''Be careful what you wish for, Danny boy,'' his uncle said softly. ''You might not like what you get.''

Dan digested his uncle's words of warning. The meaning behind the well-known cliché became clearer with each passing moment.

What if through the passage of time, he had turned Victoria into a larger-than-life romantic image? And, more to the point, no matter what had occurred between them before, what if she actually didn't want to have anything more to do with him?

As for her daughter; what if Victoria did finally admit Caroline Bernard was his natural child? How would that change his relationship with Victoria…or the baby?

No wonder she was afraid of him.

Dan glanced over at his uncle. His can of Guinness forgotten, his head was thrown back and his eyes were closed. Asleep? Dan shook his head. No, he thought fondly, his uncle was more than likely waiting for him to decide to do what was right.

Dan suddenly realized the most important player in this game was little Caroline, not Victoria and certainly not him. The baby had had a father who loved her. A man who had provided her with a loving home and family name. What did he, as a single man with a naval career as a lawyer, have to offer the little girl?

Most important, he thought as he met his uncle's now open and sympathetic gaze, how many lives might he ruin if he persisted in this insanity?

Maybe his uncle was more on target than he knew.

"You're right, Uncle Pat," Dan finally said. "I might be right about Victoria having been the woman I met over a year ago, and about her baby being my child, but I know I have no right to do anything about it. Not at this late date."

"I have great faith in you, Danny boy," his uncle said with a smile as tears formed in the corners of his eyes. "No matter how much this child might mean to you, I know in the end you'll do the right thing."

IT WAS nearing midnight when Dan finally strode up to the front door of the embassy, the Bernard family photograph hidden under his tuxedo jacket. When he rang and waited for admittance, he was prompted to remember the tale of Cinderella. Would he turn into a pumpkin at the stroke of midnight? Would he be exposed for the jackass he was about to make out of himself?

Strike that, he thought as he identified himself to the man at the front door. Make it the jackass that he *had* been before his uncle had helped him put his head on straight. Now that he'd decided to leave the past where it belonged, he was a changed man.

He had to return the photograph to the library

tonight without anyone seeing him do it. Then he had to leave, even if he couldn't say goodbye to Victoria.

When the guard at the door asked to see his invitation, Dan told him he'd already been inside and had come back to pick up something he'd forgotten. All he got was a raised eyebrow.

He was about to ask for May Stevens when he recalled Mike telling him about the ominous e-mail the embassy had received threatening Victoria and Caroline. There was no way he could afford to involve the former duchess to gain entry without violating his promise to Admiral Crowley not to create another international incident as his friend Wade Stevens had done when he'd rescued May. At least Wade had married his duchess, he thought wryly. *He* was going leave empty-handed.

And he didn't want May to use her royal status to stir up the authorities. The last thing Victoria needed was to wind up in the morning papers.

Dan finally settled for asking to speak to Mike Wheeler, the Secret Service agent who was assisting the embassy's special forces to guard the embassy and its guests tonight.

How in the hell was he going to explain his previous departure to Mike without looking like a fool? he wondered. More to the point, how was he going to explain having to go back to the library so he could return the photograph he'd ''borrowed''?

By the time Mike Wheeler finally showed, Dan's

nerves were as taut as violin strings. After looking at the grim expression in Wheeler's eyes, he was damn sure he'd never make a good criminal, let alone a good spy.

"Back again?" Wheeler nodded to the door's guardian to allow Dan to pass. "I'm glad you're here," he went on as he motioned Dan inside. "I wanted to talk to you."

"Why?" Dan tore his gaze away from where Victoria Bernard stood across the room talking to a guest. The man had a tuxedoed chest covered with medals and honorary awards and, to Dan's disgust, a haughty manner to match. Dan snorted. Experience with the military had taught him that the more medals a man wore, the lower he and his country were on the diplomatic totem pole. The man was a phony and worth keeping an eye on. The expression on Victoria's face told him she wasn't thrilled with her current company, either.

"...because I still don't understand why you would want to apologize to your hostess for simply coming here uninvited, that's why," he heard Mike explain. "Anyway, I understood the duchess invited you."

Dan's eyes widened. "You had *me* checked out? I thought we were friends."

"Friendship has nothing to do with it when I'm on duty." Mike Wheeler fixed him with a calculating look. "My take on all of this is that there's something more behind all of this 'apology' business than the lack of a written invitation. Am I right?''

When Dan realized it wasn't a good idea to enlist Mike's help in getting back to the library, or telling him of his suspicions about the ersatz general, he shrugged. He looked around the room for another means to get inside the library without Mike's help.

As he glanced across the room looking for an inspiration, he noticed Victoria's gaze seemed to have settled on him.

''Pardon me,'' he told Mike, ''I think I'll go on over and join the conversation.'' He motioned to the group of people around Victoria. ''And, by the way, thanks for speaking up for me.''

''Just don't do anything to make me regret it,'' Mike growled as his gaze followed Dan's. ''On the other hand, you might want to save your thanks until after I see if the lady wants to talk to you.''

As soon as Victoria saw Dan O'Hara and Mike Wheeler make their way across the floor toward her, mental warning bells sounded. She'd already decided to try to settle things with Dan before asking him to leave and never to come back. Mike Wheeler's presence at Dan's side made her uneasy. The fewer people who knew about her long-ago romantic involvement with Dan, the better.

She'd made her decision actually to talk to Dan because she was tired of running away from the truth and she was tired of avoiding him. It was time to take charge of her future or run the risk of losing it all.

It wasn't the long-ago midnight encounter with Dan that worried her. She'd told her late husband about that night when she'd agreed to marry him. What she had never told him was the name of the man involved…Dan O'Hara.

It was her daughter she had to protect, she told herself. Caroline was Rolande's child, she told herself firmly; she'd never allow anyone to take that away from Caroline or to sully her reputation. She also intended to make it clear to Dan that any chance of a further involvement between them was impossible. She had her diplomatic position to think of. If it came down to a choice between her country and Dan, it was no contest. No matter what her heart told her

She made her excuses to General Leontov and made her way across the room to meet Dan and Mike, stopping to greet guests along the way. "Are you enjoying the evening, gentlemen?"

"Yes, thank you," Mike answered as he gazed around a room filled with well-dressed men and women trying to impress each other. "If trouble is brewing, so far there hasn't been any sign of it. Everyone looks happy enough."

"Yes, they seem to be." Victoria smiled to cover her apprehension. Happy? She hadn't known a minute of peace from the time Dan had reappeared in her life. Just when she'd finally reconciled herself to a chaste existence as a widow, Dan had appeared. Now her thoughts and her life were in turmoil. "I checked upstairs about an hour ago. Caroline is asleep." She turned her gaze on Dan. "The doorman told me you wanted to speak to me?"

Dan glanced at Mike who, for some reason, remained at his side. Whatever was bothering the Secret Service agent, he wasn't saying, but his reservations about Dan's presence were clear.

"Are you sure you want to talk to Dan, Mrs. Bernard? If not, I'll just…"

"Yes, I do, Mike. Thank you. I'll see you later." Victoria drew a lace shawl that matched her gown closer around her shoulders and looked at Dan. "Perhaps in the library?"

Dan nodded. He had to forget how Victoria's glance made his senses stir, his body react. He had to forget that chance encounter long ago in the fairy-tale country of Baronovia. He had to remember that his goal of getting the photograph back into its frame was getting closer. The trick would be to do it without alarming Victoria.

"If you're sure," Mike Wheeler agreed reluctantly. "I'll just check around a bit, but I won't be far away. If you want me, just holler." He glanced at his watch and pointedly looked at Dan.

Dan kept an innocent expression on his face, but his heart was pounding like mad. It was obvious Wheeler didn't buy his apology. His showing up here twice in one night only added to the man's suspicions. With his uncle Pat's warning to be careful what he wished for in the back of his mind, Dan vowed to make a clean break with Victoria, to move on with his life and to allow Victoria to get on with hers.

Victoria led the way to the library, motioned Dan inside, then closed the door behind him.

She sat down behind the desk and folded her trembling hands in her lap. "Now that we're alone, we might as well be open with each other. You don't intend to forget we knew each other, do you?"

"No," he said, his body responding to Victoria in spite of himself. "You're not a woman a man can easily forget."

When he saw the anguish come into Victoria's eyes, he hurried ahead. "Don't worry. Everything has changed since the last time we spoke. I think…"

"It's not what *you* think that matters, Mr. O'Hara. It's what *I* think." She motioned Dan to a seat. "What will it take to make you forget me?"

As she spoke, Victoria steeled herself to look squarely into Dan's eyes without giving away the turmoil welling up inside her.

From the first time she'd met Dan again, she'd known she had to make a choice. A choice between the man with whom, against all reason, she seemed to have fallen in love, and the respectful life as Baronovia's ambassador she'd made for herself. She had to choose between her love for Dan and her love for her daughter. That was a choice that was no choice at all.

As for Caroline, since the baby was too young to make her choice, she had to make it for her.

"I was a foolish woman that night in Baronovia, Mr. O'Hara," she went on. "But the woman who so foolishly gave herself to you doesn't exist any longer—if she existed at all. You must forget you ever met her."

"Forget you?" Dan leaned forward and met her gaze across the desk. "How can I forget you when every time I see you I remember how wonderful you felt in my arms?"

The longing in Dan's eyes sent swift warm currents of desire coursing through her. She had to force herself to meet his eyes. "Then I shall have to make it a point to stay out of your arms, Mr. O'Hara, won't I?"

"Dan," he corrected absently as if he hadn't heard her. "You've changed the color of your hair."

"What I've done doesn't matter," she said as her heart dropped another notch. "What matters is that I'm asking you never to speak of this again."

She had to look away from Dan's clear blue eyes, his golden hair and the features her daughter had inherited. As she glanced around the desk, desire for Dan turned into dismay. The frame that held her favorite family picture was empty!

She glanced wildly around the room for the missing photograph and back at the empty frame. Before she could reach for the telephone, Dan broke in. "I assume you're looking for this?" He drew the missing photograph from his tuxedo jacket and set it on the desk in front of her.

"How did you get it?" Victoria stared at the photograph and looked as if her world was about to crumble. "What have you done?" she whispered.

"It's not what you think," he hurried to explain. "I took the photograph to show to my uncle."

"Your uncle?" Victoria's hands were shaking as she tried to insert the photograph back into its ornate metal frame. "What does your uncle have to do with the picture of my family?"

Instead of trying to put the photograph back in its frame, she finally held it close to her breast as if she feared he would try to take it from her.

"I wanted to show the photograph to my uncle Pat. He's the only one who knew me as a small child."

"What does that have to do with anything?"

"You know why, Victoria," he said quietly. "I wanted to know if he agreed with me that Caroline could be my child. It isn't only having to admit you know me that you've been afraid of all along," Dan went on. "You're more afraid of me for your daughter's sake. You're afraid I would find out I'm Caroline's father."

Victoria shook her head, but the growing despair in her eyes gave her away.

"Tell me the truth and I promise you I'll leave and never come back," he said. "I have to know."

"You don't have to know anything!"

"Then tell me the truth because I *deserve* to know."

Victoria jumped to her feet and, still holding the photograph, pointed to the door. "Please leave before I call for someone to remove you!"

When Dan's blue eyes seemed to take on a deeper hue with emotion, Victoria suddenly understood how selfish she was. The man she'd loved and lost was entitled to know his own child. Just as her child was entitled to know her real father.

She bit back the instinct to use Rolande's name to deny the truth. Even if he hadn't known the name of Caroline's natural father, Rolande had known and had accepted the truth of Caroline's conception before they were married. Did she owe Caroline's natural father anything less than the truth?

"Oh, Dan," she sighed as she lovingly replaced the picture in the frame photograph on the desk. "Our meeting that night long ago was nothing more than a passing moment. I was too young and inexperienced to know what I was doing. I'm a different person now, as are you."

"Maybe." Dan gazed into her eyes as if he could find the truth there. Where he was able to find his answer was in the color of her hair. No matter how she denied it, it was clear to him Victoria had dyed her hair in order to look like Caroline.

"Before I go," he said impulsively, "I have to ask. Did you love your husband?"

"It's not a question you have the right to ask," she said quietly, "but, yes, I did. Rolande made me see that love can be more than the physical joining of two people. He taught me love means caring for someone more than you care for yourself. He was a very devoted father."

"Then I guess I qualify for knowing what love means," Dan replied amid the growing realization he cared more for Victoria's happiness and Caroline's future than he cared for his own. He turned to leave.

"Why couldn't you have left well enough alone?" Victoria cried after him. "Why did you have to come here tonight?

"I had to," he answered in the quiet voice that had already torn her heart into hundreds of smaller pieces. "I only wanted to hear you say Caroline is my daughter. She might need me one day."

The anguish on Victoria's face and in her body language were all the answers he needed. He gazed at her for the last time and left her.

The need to have Victoria admit he was Caroline's natural father somehow no longer seemed that important. What was more important was that what had started out as a challenge had turned into a voyage of self-discovery, of learning the meaning of true love and sacrifice.

He recognized true love now. Recognition had

come at the moment Victoria had been willing to sacrifice her own identity in order to protect her child by concealing the identity of her child's natural father.

Chapter Nine

Back in his own apartment Dan paced the floor like a caged tiger. He hadn't wanted to leave the embassy before he came to an understanding with Victoria, but he'd known better than to insist. He'd had to leave. If he'd remained, Mike Wheeler would have eventually gotten around to asking questions he didn't want to answer. Questions he couldn't answer, not without possibly harming Victoria and jeopardizing her daughter's future.

To add to his frustration, the photograph he'd "borrowed" clearly showed Rolande Bernard had cared for Caroline. The loving expression in the man's eyes as he'd gazed at the baby had been undeniable.

It was clear from the photo that Bernard, Victoria and Caroline had been a family.

The idea of claiming Caroline as his child was ridiculous.

The baby had to be better off with her widowed

mother than with a single man like himself who had always put his duties as a naval lawyer first, he told himself. A man whose duties at JAG could take him all over the world was no father at all.

There had to be an explanation for being drawn to the idea of having a child—Caroline. Maybe it had been because he'd been an only child. Maybe it had been the early deaths of his own parents overseas in a train accident. He'd been adopted by his uncle, sure, but Pat had been away a great deal of the time. For too many months the only parent he'd known had been Rose, his uncle's housekeeper, a woman who had given him unconditional love.

Sure, he'd finally gotten around to drawing up a five-year plan for the future, he told himself, but it had come too late. Too late for it to include Victoria and Caroline.

Finally realizing how weary he was and the futility of his thoughts, he prepared to undress. The doorbell rang. Surprised that there could be anyone out there at this late hour, he made for the door. A look through the peephole brought him up short. It was Mike Wheeler. Behind him were two stalwart D.C. policemen.

His first thought was that there was a crisis involving Victoria. He threw open the door. "It's two o'clock in the morning, Mike! Something wrong?"

"I need you back at the embassy for a chat." Wheeler gestured at his two silent sidekicks. "You can volunteer to come peaceably, or I can roust out a judge to obtain a summons. Either way…''

"Hold on!" Dan shivered as a cold gust of foreboding enveloped him and chilled him to the bone. "I'll go with you, but not before you tell me what this is all about. I'm a lawyer, so I know the drill."

"And I don't have to be a lawyer to know I can hold you for twenty-four hours on suspicion," Mike replied dryly. "If you'd rather, we can arrest you and start with your Miranda rights."

"Miranda rights!" A storm of anger enveloped Dan as his gaze locked with Wheeler's. Who was the man kidding? As an officer of the court, Dan had a healthy respect for the law. He'd kept his nose clean, well, most of the time, yet here was Mike Wheeler, a man whom he'd thought of as a friend until tonight, treating him like a common criminal!

"On suspicion of what? And furthermore," Dan went on, trying to keep a lid on his temper, "why do we need to go back to the embassy at this time of night?"

"I figured the surroundings would help you to recall facts, that's why. Of course," Wheeler added dryly, "if you'd rather talk down at the station house, I'm sure these gentlemen would be happy to oblige."

Before Dan could cool down, Wheeler whipped a card from his pocket and, with a businesslike glance at Dan, began to read. "You have the right to remain silent…"

"Hell!" Disgusted and angry enough to take a swing at Wheeler, Dan headed for the bedroom. "You can go ahead and read whatever you want to, but I'm not going anywhere before I change."

His mind on what possible crime he could have committed to bring on the gendarmes, Dan took off his tuxedo and pleated shirt and whipped on slacks, a warm flannel shirt and a jacket. "If you really believe I'm guilty of something, you're out of your mind," he muttered into Wheeler's enigmatic expression.

"Maybe." Wheeler shrugged when he was through reading, but Dan knew better. Wheeler was dead serious about something. It was the "something" that began to bother him. "Ready?"

The ride in the unmarked sedan was made in an uneasy silence. The only thing that kept Dan from trying to pump Wheeler were those dammed Miranda rights and Wheeler's raised eyebrows whenever Dan glanced in his direction.

Once back at the embassy, Wheeler escorted Dan to the library. He motioned the two policemen to wait outside, closed the door behind him and sailed into Dan.

"Now, how would you like to tell me one more time about why you felt you had to show up at the embassy? Tonight of all nights?"

"I've already told you why." Stealing a glance to see if the Bernard family photograph was back on the desk, Dan prowled the room. His blood ran cold when Wheeler's glance followed his. Cursing himself for forgetting Wheeler was a Secret Service agent first and a friend second, he hurriedly glanced away.

"Tell me again."

To add to Dan's unease, his stomach was churning and a roaring headache was about to take off the top of his head. Wheeler wasn't helping

Dan gritted his teeth. With his career on the line if it became known he was in the custody of the law, he was in no mood to cooperate with anyone. Reason won out when he realized he had three choices. He could cooperate with Wheeler, be interrogated by the embassy's special forces or be turned over to the tender, loving mercy of the D.C. police. Any way he looked at it, he was behind the eight ball and still counting.

"Like I said, I came here tonight to apologize to Victoria for upsetting her the other day when we were all at your house," Dan said wearily. No way was he going to tell Mike about his prior encounter with Victoria at the Stevens's housewarming. And he sure as hell wasn't prepared to tell the man about his earlier encounter with Victoria back in Baronovia. Better to pretend they had been two strangers when they met at Wheeler's.

"Upsetting her about…?"

"I'm not at liberty to say. It's a private matter between the two of us," Dan said. "Would you be satisfied if I told you we had just settled it tonight?"

"No." Wheeler didn't look impressed. The cool look on his face continued to make Dan uneasy. If there had been any measure of friendship between the two of them, it sure was gone now.

"That's only one of the things I wanted to talk about," Mike said with a grim look that sent Dan's blood pressure sky-high. He gestured to a chair. "Sit."

With the realization there would be more to this interview, Dan fought his frustration and sat. He'd been around crime and criminals long enough to feel the negative vibrations coming at him and it wasn't a comforting feeling. "So, if it's not just me, what is wrong?"

"Plenty." Wheeler stared at him so intently that the hair on the back of Dan's neck began to prickle.

"What's 'plenty'?" All his senses on alert, Dan slowly rose to his feet. He hadn't liked the way the "interview" had been going before this, and he liked it even less now.

"We had a small fire—a kitchen fire. Discovered it after you left."

"Good God! Anyone hurt?" Dan's first instinct was that Victoria and the baby had been injured in the fire. He jumped from his chair and started toward the door.

"No. The fire wasn't big enough to burn the place down." Wheeler moved in front of the door, his gaze fixed on Dan as if to judge his reaction. "But there was enough smoke blowing through the air-conditioning vents to have us clear the embassy.''

Dan fought his frustration and growing anger. He recalled noticing a clean-up crew at work when he'd been escorted inside. "That's good to hear, but what does that have to do with me?"

Wheeler's silence and steady questioning gaze almost drove Dan to grab him by his collar and shake the story out of him.

"Jeez!" Dan exclaimed. "I've had it! Either tell me why I'm here or let me go."

Wheeler's gaze rested on Dan for a long moment. "Might as well tell you, since you're going to find out for yourself anyway. It's more than the fire." Without waiting for Dan to react, the agent went on. "After the fire started, Victoria went upstairs again to check on her daughter. The baby's crib was empty."

The implication behind Wheeler's statement finally hit Dan. Not only had Caroline been taken by someone, Wheeler obviously thought he was the someone.

"Go on," Dan said, clenching and unclenching his fists. Losing his temper wasn't going to get him anywhere.

"Caroline is missing," Wheeler continued, "and so is the woman who was watching over her, Lydia Monsour."

To Dan's dismay, the agent's eyes narrowed. "But then, you already knew that, didn't you?"

Dan felt himself blanch. Mike Wheeler *was* actually looking at him as though he had something to do with the baby's disappearance. Kidnapping his own daughter?

He surged to his feet. "You're out of your cotton-picking mind!" He'd clenched his fists to keep from using Wheeler as a punching bag when the reasons behind why Wheeler suspected him of the kidnapping hit him.

Could Victoria have told Wheeler that he was Caroline's natural father and that was why he was under suspicion? "What does Victoria think about your theory?"

Wheeler shrugged. "Didn't have time to run it by her, but I intend to."

Dan bit his lower lip. If Wheeler was waiting for Dan to say something, anything that would incriminate him, he was out of luck. "You'd better have a damn good reason for trying to pin this on me, Mike! First a fire, now a missing baby! Why in the hell aren't you out there looking for the guilty party?"

"Because, considering the circumstances, we're starting with the most logical suspect. You."

"Me? Hell, I wasn't even here!" Dan eyed the closed door and tried to figure the odds of persuading Mike Wheeler to let him go long enough to do some checking around on his own. "Are you saying that after the embassy had received e-mails threatening Victoria and her daughter there were no guards upstairs who could have prevented this from happening?''

A look of disgust passed over Wheeler's face. The lack of reliable guards was obviously a sore spot. ''There were two,'' he said with a grimace. ''I understand they were downstairs in the kitchen checking out the fire.''

Dan's eyes narrowed. ''Since when do both bodyguards leave at the same time?''

''Hell, they weren't my men,'' said Wheeler, looking disgusted as Dan felt. ''They were part of the embassy's special forces. My men have been trained never to leave a charge alone.''

''That's good to know,'' Dan remarked facetiously. ''Someone else had to be watching the baby,'' he went on, mentally cursing his own inability to have had the right to keep Caroline safe from harm.

''The only other person in the family living quarters was the nanny and she's still out like a light.''

''Why pick on me as the kidnapper? Why aren't you out there looking for the real suspects?''

Wheeler's eyes narrowed. ''What makes you think there was more than one kidnapper?''

''For God's sakes! It was only a figure of speech!'' Dan eyed the agent with disgust. ''I still think you need to be out there investigating instead of wasting your time on me.''

''What makes you think we're not?''

Dan knew where that left him. Either Wheeler

suspected he was the kidnapper, or Wheeler believed that Dan had contracted someone to commit the crime for him. If Wheeler knew or suspected he was Caroline's natural father, he sure as hell would be number one on the most-wanted list. It was Dan's guess that his name topped the list already.

Wheeler considered him for a long, suspenseful moment, long enough for Dan to believe he was about to experience the ignominy of being hauled off to jail. "I have some of my men and the embassy's security forces spread out looking for clues. But that's beside the point. Right now, I want to know the real reasons you came here tonight." Mike added ominously, "Why you left, and why you came back two hours later. I don't buy it that it was just to talk to Victoria Bernard."

"Why don't you ask the lady?" Disgusted, Dan resumed prowling the library. Each time he passed the desk, he fought to keep his eyes off the framed photograph on the desk.

"I will as soon as she wakes up."

"Wakes up?" Dan froze. "Victoria hasn't been hurt, has she?"

"No, not really. The doctor gave her a light sedative to calm her down."

At Wheeler's answer, Dan's frustration lit up again, this time like a bonfire. His first instinct had been to find Victoria. To reassure her he was innocent of the kidnapping and to offer his assistance to find the little girl he was sure was his child. Now he was helpless.

Since it looked as if Victoria might have been the one who had turned the finger of suspicion on him, his chances of getting out of here without being charged were beginning to look about as good as a snowball's chances in hell.

He clenched his hands to keep from punching the suspicious look off Mike's face. "I keep telling you. I only came to apologize to Victoria. I had nothing to do with her daughter's disappearance." Outwardly calm, Dan's insides were churning.

"Not good enough." Wheeler shook his head.

"That's all there is to tell. The next thing I know, you'll probably say I started the kitchen fire to distract the gendarmes long enough to take the kid away, or to hire someone to do it."

"You said it." Wheeler's satisfied smile didn't reach his eyes. The ensuing silence between the two was thick enough to cut with a knife. Finally Dan realized his temper had run away with him.

"I did not have anything to do with the baby's kidnapping," he repeated slowly and emphatically. "I swear it!"

"Could be, but I doubt it," Wheeler finally said. "The fire made a good cover for you, wouldn't you say?"

Dan bit back a curse. "Is there any way I can convince you I had nothing to do with Caroline Bernard's disappearance? That I only came back here for private reasons?''

''No. Not after your two-hour absence. Besides,'' Wheeler added forcefully, ''there's nothing private in a kidnapping! And especially not when a child is involved!''

It was all Dan could do to keep himself from demanding to talk to Victoria. ''If you have to know,'' he said when he realized he had to tell as much of the truth as he could, ''I was gone for such a long time because I wanted to visit my uncle before I came back.''

''First a disagreement with Mrs. Bernard and now an uncle? Any other cockamammy alibis?''

''It's not an alibi, dammit,'' Dan spit out. ''Do I look like someone who would start a fire to distract you long enough to take a kid?'' Even as he spoke he knew there were a lot of guilty people out there who looked more innocent than he did. ''But that's besides the point. You're wasting a hell of a lot of precious time, man! The longer we stay here arguing, the farther away the people who took this woman Lydia and the baby could get!''

The library door suddenly burst open with a bang against the wall and a distraught Victoria Bernard burst into the room. When she saw Dan, she ran to him and grasped him by his jacket lapels. ''Where is my baby? What have you done with her?''

Speechless, Dan grabbed her hands. ''I swear I

didn't have anything to do with it. I didn't take Caroline!''

Fighting tears, Victoria shook her head. ''If you really care for me, please tell me the truth. Did you take Caroline to get even with me?''

Dan caught a glimpse of a satisfied expression crossing Mike Wheeler's face. Instantly Dan realized he no longer had a chance of convincing anyone he was innocent, if there had been the chance to begin with. Not when Victoria was practically accusing him of being involved.

A hollow feeling came over Dan. He realized he was teetering on the edge of becoming involved in something larger than a possible diplomatic incident. This was now a highly person matter, but the repercussions could affect not only himself but the United States government.

Angry and hurt, Dan mentally cursed the fate that had brought him here. All he'd wanted in the beginning was to have Victoria confirm she was his mystery lady. The part about the baby being his natural child had come later.

He grasped Victoria's hands in his, locked her gaze with his and willed her to believe him. ''I swear to you that I didn't have anything to do with Caroline's disappearance!''

''How can I believe you?'' Victoria sobbed, the anguish in her voice breaking his heart. ''You are the only one with a motive for taking Caroline away from me!''

"On my honor as a human being and an officer of the court, I swear it's the truth." Dan wanted to remind her he'd already told her he was sorry his questions about his role in her past had tormented her, but Wheeler was listening and waiting to discover a motive behind the kidnapping. Dan wanted to tell her that, after guessing he was Caroline's natural father, he'd decided not to pressure her to tell the truth—even though he had guessed it. How could she even think he would get back at her this way? Why wouldn't she believe him?

"If you let me, I'll help you find her."

Wheeler stepped closer to him. Dan waved him off, silently pleading for more time.

Victoria's tears hardened Dan's resolve to help find Caroline. Nine years of practicing law had to amount to something, he told himself as he glanced at Wheeler. The first step would be to get this man, embassy security and the D.C. police off his back.

He gazed down into Victoria's tear-filled eyes. In another time and in a different place, he would have taken her in his arms and erased those tears with his lips, his kisses. He would have shown her how much he'd grown to love her and respect her. He felt too deeply for her to cause her such pain. He would have told her he intended to make sure her beautiful and vulnerable eyes should never have to weep again.

Certainly not because of him.

"I swear I'll find your daughter for you, Victoria," he said softly. "Believe it."

He glanced over Victoria's head at a watchful Mike Wheeler. With the odds already piled up against his innocence, he was damn sure Wheeler wouldn't allow him to call the shots, let alone be allowed to participate in the search for any clues to the identity of the kidnapper.

"Can you prove you have nothing to do with Caroline's disappearance?" she whispered.

"I will, but I'm afraid it looks as if I may be under arrest any minute," he told Victoria as he stopped himself from brushing away the tears from her flushed cheeks. "In fact," he added between heavy heartbeats, "I've already been read my rights. I feel as if I already have my hands handcuffed behind my back."

In the background he heard Wheeler snort at the handcuff remark. The interpretation was clear. If Wheeler had his way, the next thing would be the sound of handcuffs around his wrists and iron doors closing behind him. "Is there a chance you can do something about getting rid of my escort?"

Victoria fought back her tears. The resolve and strength she saw in Dan's clear blue eyes was undeniable. His expression was tender. No man could lie and look so compassionate at the same time. He had to be telling her the truth.

The physical attraction between them was still there, she thought sadly as she despaired of ever coming to grips with the way she felt about Dan. In spite of her resolve to put him in the past where he belonged, it seemed that their mutual attraction grew stronger every time they met, even now, as her heart threatened to break.

But was she able to trust him?

In order to trust him, she told herself, she had to give him a chance. Under the circumstances it seemed that her only chance to let him prove he wasn't the kidnapper was to have him set free. But she would stick by his side until her precious Caroline was returned to her.

Her heart was heavy, but she made up her mind to try to do as he asked. If it became a choice between letting Wheeler take Dan in or having him free to find Caroline, there was no choice at all.

An inner voice demanded she make the commonsense decision. She knew deep in her heart that by now Dan had to know Caroline was his child. That he would do anything and everything in his power to bring her back. She had to believe in him.

"I will speak to the authorities, Mr. O'Hara," she finally agreed. "However, I must warn you, whatever you plan on doing, wherever you go, I insist on being there with you. I couldn't live with myself if I just waited here."

Dan started to object, to tell her she was better off waiting here, until he realized that, as a Baronovian national, Victoria had the diplomatic immunity he needed to get into places he couldn't go alone. If it came down to that, she could invoke that immunity to get the law off his back. With her at his side, he could ask questions he might not have the right to ask and, above all, get answers.

He dropped his hands and reluctantly nodded his agreement. "Okay," he said, even as he silently prayed he was doing the right thing.

First, he had to get his act together. "Since it's already too late to get much done tonight, if it's okay with you, I'll start by looking around Caroline's room. Next, I figure on asking the staff some questions and maybe coming up with answers that will help."

Wheeler cleared his throat. "Not so fast, Dan. As far as I'm concerned, you're still mine."

"I don't think so," Dan said. "As I understand international law, the embassy is considered to be foreign territory. As long as I'm in the embassy, I'm off the hook for now."

Wheeler had to know the facts as well as he did, Dan thought, as his heart thudded wildly beneath his ribs in anticipation of Wheeler's counterargument. God forbid there was some way for Wheeler and the U.S. Secret Service to find a way to get around that law.

Obviously frustrated, Wheeler glanced at him, then at Victoria. "Guess the man is right," he said reluctantly. "For now."

Dan didn't like the "for now" but he wasn't going to challenge Mike, until he was home free. Right now he needed to be free of Wheeler's clutches to have the chance to find Caroline.

Just as he was congratulating himself, Victoria's father burst into the room. "What is going on here?"

"Father." Victoria quickly went to his side. "Mr. O'Hara has asked to help us find Caroline. I agreed."

"No," Basil Esterhazy said firmly. "I refuse to let this matter leave the embassy premises. The last thing I want is for our embassy and my family to be splashed all over the newspapers and on television! We are a new embassy and have a reputation to consider."

His eyes were cold as he surveyed the room. "We are going to handle this without the Secret Service—" he glanced at Wheeler "—or the local police, and we will do it before the newspapers get hold of the story. Mr. Wheeler and Mr. O'Hara must leave!"

Victoria gasped. "Father, wait! You can't mean that! Every minute Caroline is gone is crucial to our finding her! Surely Caroline is more important than the embassy's reputation!"

"You are mistaken, my dear. I intend to find Caroline," he assured her, "but with the help of our own people."

Victoria looked helplessly at her father. "If you won't accept outside help, at least allow Dan to remain and help search for the baby." When he looked as if he was about to balk, she added, "Dan is a friend of May and her husband. He and Wade are both lawyers in the navy."

Dan simmered while the ambassador considered his daughter's plea. He sensed Victoria's father was reluctant and even puzzled at her request—until he saw Esterhazy glance at the framed photograph on his desk and back to him.

Dan kept himself under control, his features impassive. No way could he afford to give his suspected relationship with Caroline away.

"What kind of help do you propose to provide, Mr. O'Hara?"

"My experience in the U.S. Navy's Judge Advocate General's Corps, sir," Dan said pragmatically. With the man already suspicious, giving any personal reasons for wanting to help in the search for the baby was out of the question. "This wouldn't be my first investigation into a kidnapping," he added, before he went on, "I plan on taking a leave of absence, so that any help I can provide will be strictly as private citizen. I assure you that no federal or local police agencies will be involved, at least not by me."

Apparently satisfied, Victoria's father nodded. His gaze turned to Victoria. "You wish this?"

"Yes, father, I do," she said. "Very much!"

"Then Mr. O'Hara can stay. But please remember I intend to keep this matter within these walls. The Secret Service and local police must leave!"

Dan clenched his hands at the horror that had come over Victoria's face during her exchange with her father. He had to force himself to remain silent at the realization that the man's position as the embassy's chargé d'affaires came before the man's family.

"My decision is final, Victoria," Basil Esterhazy said again as if for emphasis. "We will find Caroline by ourselves." He turned to Mike Wheeler who stood nearby in disbelief. "I appreciate your help tonight, Mr. Wheeler, but it is time to remove yourself and your men. Please take the local police with you."

"Are you sure about that, sir?" Wheeler protested. "If we wait to start the search, possible clues may be disturbed."

"My decision is final. If there are any questions, you may have your superior call me in the morning."

Victoria stared at her father as if he were a stranger. The kind and gentle man she would have trusted with her life had turned out to be a mindless autocrat whose first concern appeared to be Baronovia's reputation instead of his granddaughter's safety. Holding back her tears, she glanced over at Dan. Dan had been the man she'd been afraid of, but had turned out to be the man she *could* trust.

Chapter Ten

"Victoria?" Basil Esterhazy waited until Mike Wheeler had thrown up his hands and strode out of the room. The tension in the room became thicker when Esterhazy turned to Victoria. "You will do as I say?"

Heartsick, Victoria gazed at her father, a stranger she no longer recognized as the loving father she'd always known. She wanted to protest, to ask him to reconsider, to allow outside help, but the unyielding look in his eyes told her his mind was made up. At least he had left her Dan, she thought. As Caroline's father, openly or not, Dan had as much at stake as she did in finding Caroline.

"Whatever you say, Father," she answered quietly. "As long as we begin to search for Caroline immediately. I intend to help in the search."

"So be it," he answered with a frown. "But only as long as you and Mr. O'Hara keep me informed. I have instructed the staff to report back here to me later. I have to prepare for a very important meeting first thing in the morning, or I would accompany you.'' He gazed at her for a long moment, then, apparently satisfied, turned to Dan. ''Mr. O'Hara, please do not touch or move anything until I join you.'' He placed a perfunctory kiss on Victoria's cheek and left.

Her safe world as she knew it in pieces, Victoria sadly watched her father leave the room. She turned back to Dan who stood staring out the large picture window, deep in thought.

She followed his gaze to the outdoor lights that now lit up the embassy gardens. The lights shone on a fountain where the cascading water turned into shining blue-and-white diamonds. Two stone doves perched on the rim.

To add to Victoria's dismay, the scene was almost a duplicate of the fountain in the palace grounds in Baronovia. The very place where she and Dan had first met and she had given herself to him.

She was about to address Dan as Mr. O'Hara when she realized the futility of trying to behave as if he were a stranger.

''Dan?'' she said softly. ''What are your plans?''

Dan turned away from the window. His expression was carefully guarded, but his eyes gave him away. She knew he had to have been reminded of another night and another place, just as she had been. Sick with worry about her missing daughter, she hid the emotions his eyes stirred within her.

"I don't intend to wait for your father's return, Victoria. With or without his consent, I intend to get started right away."

"*We* can get started," she corrected grimly. She sat down at the desk and removed a yellow legal pad and pen from the center drawer. "I intend to work with you."

He dropped into a chair alongside the desk and, for a moment, looked as if he was going to protest. "If that's what you really want to do," he finally said, shrugging.

Dan's cool gaze was welcome, Victoria thought gratefully as she glanced at the framed photograph on the desk. The more distant Dan became, the easier it would be to keep from remembering how important he had become to her.

"If you're ready," he said, gesturing to the pad of paper on the desk. "We can start with a list of everyone who has daily access to Caroline."

"The chauffeur, Stefan," she said thoughtfully and wrote down the name.

"Why Stefan?"

"He watches me so closely, especially when my daughter is with me. He makes me feel as if I am a prisoner." She shuddered and bit her lower lip.

"Have you mentioned this to your father?"

"No, not yet. Actually," she added with a faint smile, "I did dismiss him whenever I could, but I felt a little foolish. After all, he was just doing his job. I guess I just didn't like the way he was doing it.''

''Nothing is foolish at times like these,'' Dan assured her. ''I'll look into this man, Stefan, but I suggest you tell your father right away. Who else?''

''Lydia Monsour,'' she went on reluctantly, ''but that is a foolish choice. When I was a child, Lydia was my beloved nanny. She has remained with me as my dear friend and companion.''

''How foolish can it be to list her when the woman *is* missing?'' Dan gestured to the yellow lined pad. ''Put her name down, anyway.''

''I know.'' Victoria frowned and wrote down Lydia's name.

''Who else?''

''Caroline's nanny, Elise, but she can't possibly be involved. The poor dear was drugged by the kidnapper!''

''That doesn't mean she's innocent,'' Dan said dryly. ''The attack on the woman could be part of a cover-up. Better put her name on the list. If we're going to get anywhere, we have to start with all the people closest to Caroline.''

Horrified, Victoria stared at him. ''Neither Lydia or Elise would harm the baby.''

''Of course not,'' Dan assured her. He went back to looking out the window. ''No one is going to harm a hair on Caroline's head, if I have anything to do with it. It's more likely the baby is going to be held for some kind of ransom. Have you or any of your family received any telephone calls or written demands for money?''

"No.'' Victoria shook her head and wrote down Elise's name. Thank God, so far the list was short.

"Can you think of anyone who may not be close to you and yet could be involved?''

"Not really. We haven't been here in your country very long.'' Victoria thought of her cousin May's earlier remark that since Dan was a citizen of the United States, Caroline was a U.S. citizen, too, and how Dan might be in a position to help Caroline if necessary. Should she remind him?

"How about one of the guests last night?'' Dan's question brought Victoria's mind back to the moment. "For instance, the general with all those ribbons and medals on his chest?''

"General Leontov,'' Victoria replied with a shudder. "He is a general in the army of Slavonia, a small country neighboring Baronovia. Although I heard Leontov was openly against our diplomatic alliance with your country, he has been silent lately. Because of his status, we invited him to the reception tonight.''

"Put his name down anyway,'' Dan said firmly. "From what I observed earlier, the man was trying too hard to be noticed. He could be covering up what might be going on elsewhere in the embassy.''

"What made you think so?'' Victoria paused in adding the man's name to the list.

"My experience in the JAG Corps,'' Dan replied

dryly. "Dealing with international intrigue comes with the territory. Sometimes it's hard to distinguish the guilty from the innocent. As a matter of fact," he added, "I'm beginning to think that the only innocent people around here could be me and you."

Victoria felt herself blush as she remembered the accusations she'd made earlier. "With the exception of Stefan and Leontov, these are people I trust," she insisted as she studied the list. "You have to be wrong."

"Your child is missing. You can't afford to leave anyone off the list."

"Not even you?" she asked.

"As I said, you have to trust me," Dan said as his gaze swept her. "You have no other choice."

His gaze locked with hers until she nodded her agreement. "I do," she said quietly. *For more reasons than you'll ever know.*

"Anyone else regularly around you and Caroline?"

"No," she answered after a thoughtful pause, "just the regular household staff. We haven't been here long enough to fully staff the embassy. I usually take care of Caroline myself when Elise and Lydia are unavailable."

Dan paced the room restlessly. The fewer the players, the easier the search for the baby, he thought before he realized it was much too simplistic a scenario to be real. "Maybe. But someone somewhere holds a grudge against you or your father. Think.''

"There's only Fritz left.''

"Fritz?'' Dan leaned forward in his seat. "Who is Fritz and what does he do around the embassy?''

"He's Lydia's nephew. In the short time he's been in this country, Fritz was my chauffeur. Stefan took over when Fritz was injured in an automobile accident. A broken leg and a sprained arm,'' she explained, "but he would never do anything like this. We are friends.''

"That's just the type you need to watch,'' Dan told her as he paced the floor again. "The way the world is now, no one can depend on friendships. How old is this Fritz?'' He leaned over Victoria's shoulder to study the list.

"Twenty, perhaps twenty-two,'' she answered, surprised to find she was too aware of Dan's proximity. She couldn't help herself. Not only was Dan her daughter's father, after so long a time he'd become real. Not only real, she thought, he was everything she admired in a man. Strong, sure and loyal.

"After we left London and came here,'' she hurried on before her sensuous thoughts took over her senses, "Fritz wanted to visit his aunt Lydia. He said he liked living here and wanted to stay. My father gave Fritz a job so he could get a green card.''

Dan tried, as he'd intended to do with each person on the list, to put himself in Fritz's position, to think the way Fritz would think. It wasn't easy, not when he was standing so close to Victoria he could feel the heat of her skin, inhale her scent of fresh gardenias. Duty, honor, he muttered to himself as he realized this was as close to Victoria as he dared to come.

He went back to concentrating on Fritz. From the way Victoria described him, Fritz was her friend. But, damn it all, *everyone* on the list appeared to be Victoria's friend. Which said a lot for Victoria's character, but didn't help him with finding Caroline.

He stopped his pacing to look at Victoria. No shrinking violet, she had shown strength in a situation that would have floored most women of her sheltered upbringing. The person Victoria was, or at least had become in the past eighteen months, had his respect and his admiration. As well as a love he didn't dare show her.

"What we have to do first is to search Caroline's room for any sign of how she was removed," he announced. He stopped to stare at Victoria. "The baby's room hasn't been disturbed, has it?"

"No. Only her nanny is allowed in there. Or Lydia and, of course, me." She closed her eyes and leaned back in the chair. "I haven't been able to go back in there."

Victoria's silken hair was inches away from where he stood. Desire rose, his body stirred, his arms ached to hold her. More than ever, Dan wanted to take Victoria in his arms and comfort her. And even more, to wring the necks of the people who were causing her so much pain. He had to clench his fists to keep from taking her in his arms.

"I'm sorry to have to ask you to check out the baby's room," he said, "but as I see it, there's no one else who knows what should be in there. It shouldn't take long. We can go on from there to check Lydia's room for any clues to where she could have gone after we're through."

"I don't feel right about doing that, either," Victoria said unhappily. "Lydia has been closer to me than my own mother."

Dan shrugged. "Your choice, but I recommend we do it. And do it tonight."

"Dan, I…" Victoria's throat threatened to close but she forced herself to go on. She couldn't live with herself until she'd thanked Dan for helping her after she'd accused him of being the kidnapper. "…I can't tell you how much I appreciate your doing this for me."

He studied her for a long moment. Long enough for Victoria's senses to quicken at the look that had come into his eyes. The heated expression she saw there gave her a glimpse of the way he surely must feel about her.

"I owe it to you and to Caroline," he said gruffly.

"You owe me nothing!" she cried. "*I* was the one at fault for inviting you to make love to me. *I* was the one who wanted to be loved by a man of my own choice, not my father's. *I* was the one who so foolishly thought you had been sent to me and that you were my destiny.''

For a moment, Lydia thought Dan would take her in his arms and hold her in the way she yearned to be held. Not with a gentle touch or a chaste kiss, but with a deep, searching kiss that would fill her empty heart.

Dan reached to gently graze her cheek with a forefinger. ''You're torturing yourself for nothing, Victoria. It was the other way around. I was the one who was older and more experienced in what I thought was a game. It should have been obvious to me that you were caught up and acting out some kind of fantasy. I'm afraid I got caught up in it, too. I should have known better than to take advantage of you.'' He gazed at her with his heart and his emotions in his eyes laid bare for her to see. ''Have you ever been sorry?''

''How can I be sorry when I had Caroline?'' she asked softly. ''How could I be sorry when that night was the most wonderful night of my life?''

Dan held his breath as he realized what Victoria had said. Her answer was the closest she'd ever come to admitting Caroline was his child! And only, damn him for his weakness where she was concerned, because he'd taken advantage of her innate honesty and vulnerability!

He watched the realization of what she'd given away come over Victoria's face.

''Don't worry. I made a promise to you and I

intend to keep it,'' he said. "You have nothing to fear from me. I'm going to leave. I'm here now only because I intend to find Caroline.''

"And when you do?''

"And then,'' he said in a ragged voice that became stronger as he spoke, "I promise I'll get out of your life.''

Victoria's fears for her daughter tore at her heart even as she sensed what Dan's vow to take himself out of her life must have cost him.

It had to have been as much as it cost her to hear him make the vow.

Dan glanced at his watch. "I figure we have about twenty minutes before your father and the embassy staff show up. Let's go up to the nursery and look around.''

"Yes, of course,'' Victoria agreed. Visiting the empty nursery struck at her heart, but at least Dan would be with her.

Upstairs, she paused at the door to Caroline's nursery. "I'm not sure…''

The tremor in Victoria's voice and the unhappy look on her face disturbed Dan. It was as if all the strength she'd shown before now had drained from her. From the strong, fiery woman who had accused him of taking her daughter, Victoria suddenly seemed to have become a shadow of herself.

"No one knows better than you do what should be inside the room and what is missing now, Victoria. Besides,'' he added softly, his fingers aching to soothe the frown away from her forehead, "you're not alone. I'm here for you."

Dan's voice was soft and reassuring as he gazed at Victoria. If only he had the right to take her into his arms, to hold her against his heart until the lines on her forehead faded. To hold her until his strength renewed hers—until Caroline was found. And found she would be, he thought grimly as he opened the door to the nursery. With the cast of players so small and the short elapse of time since the kidnapping, he hoped they would find the baby soon.

Victoria drew a deep breath and attempted a smile, but he knew better. Her heart was elsewhere. He eyed her watchfully. "Are you going to be all right with this?"

"You're right, of course," she said, even as he sensed she would never be all right until Caroline was safely returned to her.

Victoria followed Dan into the nursery. In her imagination, she could see Caroline smiling up at her from the crib and holding out her plump little arms to be picked up.

Caroline was more than her child. She was the glue that had kept the Bernard family reputation intact; she had given meaning to her marriage bargain, a bargain that now made Victoria feel lonely and sad.

Rolande might not have been Caroline's natural father, Victoria thought as she gazed at his picture on the baby's chest of drawers, but he'd loved Caroline as if she were his own child. Rolande's love for Caroline and his unconditional love for her had made her life complete. Now, she thought with a sense of loss, she had to face the truth. Something beyond the security and affection he'd freely given her during their marriage had been missing from her life.

Maybe she shouldn't have asked Dan to stay and help find Caroline. And yet, she thought as she watched the play of emotions pass over Dan's eyes, who better to help find Caroline than her natural father?

Should she let Dan become involved in her and Caroline's lives? What would happen when everyone learned her marriage had been a sham?

She took a deep breath, and focused on looking for clues. The empty nursery was filled with the scent of baby powder and baby shampoo. The sheer yellow curtains and the upholstered window seat were fashioned of the same yellow-gold cloth as the ruffles on the baby's crib.

She stopped in midstep. There appeared to be something odd about the shadows behind the yellow curtains! She ran to the windows and pulled the curtains aside.

"Find something?" Dan was at her side in an instant.

"No," she said wearily as she turned back into the room. "I thought I saw an outline of a ladder against the window. I'm afraid I'm chasing shadows.''

Dan nodded and went to test the window. It was firmly closed, but Victoria had been right. There *was* a ladder propped up against the building. ''Looks as if someone's been washing windows. But the window seems to be firmly closed. No one could have come in and out of here without leaving some sign.''

He turned around to survey the room with a critical eye. ''As for chasing shadows, don't let that worry you. It happens all the time. Maybe one of the shadows will be a clue.

''You know, it's possible Caroline could still be inside the embassy,'' he mused, and then asked the question he would have asked long ago if he hadn't been the prime suspect—and if he hadn't been so busy trying to get away from Mike Wheeler. ''Has anyone checked the embassy building room by room for Caroline?''

''That was the first thing my father ordered after we discovered Caroline was gone and the fire was out. Why?''

''The timing of the fire points to an inside job. If so, it's possible Caroline could still be somewhere in the building.''

''No one could be that cruel,'' Victoria said, holding a tiny yellow pillow to her cheek.

''Maybe, maybe not. When the staff assembles in the library, I intend to have a serious talk with each and every one of them. Even if they're not aware of it, someone must have seen something.''

Dan glanced around the room before exclaiming, ''I don't have any experience with babies, but even I can see there's everything here a baby would need, and then some.''

''I'm afraid I spoil Caroline,'' Victoria replied, distracted by Dan's wry comment. ''Since she was going to be my only child, why wouldn't I?''

Victoria bit back a gasp at what she'd just said. Dan had been after her to admit he was Caroline's father. What would he do now that she'd twice inadvertently given him his answer?

Thankfully, she watched Dan shrug and wander off to gaze at a pile of stuffed animals sitting haphazardly on the seat of a rocking chair. ''Are all of these Caroline's?''

Thank God, Dan hadn't heard her, Victoria thought as she moved to his side. ''She loves animals. I mentioned that to Mike's wife, Charlie, the other day. That's why she invited me to bring Caroline back to visit her zoo. Remember?''

Dan looked at her wryly. ''I remember. You looked as if the world was coming to an end. I'm still not sure why you reacted like that,'' he added. ''Do you remember?''

''I remember,'' Victoria said as she tried to keep herself from remembering it hadn't only been that meeting with Dan that had upset her. The collapse of her world as she knew it had begun at their earlier introduction the night of her cousin May's house-warming. Their subsequent introduction at the Wheeler home had only hurried the process.

Victoria reluctantly moved away from Dan. No matter what Dan suspected, she had to be careful not to give away his actual relationship to her daughter. She'd been careful before, but now she felt on shaky ground. Everyone believed Rolande had been Caroline's father. Only she, Lydia and now her cousin May knew the truth.

Chapter Eleven

An icy blanket of fear covered Victoria. Had the kidnappers taken Caroline for political reasons or simply for ransom?

Was Caroline's and Lydia's disappearance somehow the beginning of a setup? A blackmailer's scheme?

What possible connection could there be between her family, Lydia and the kidnappers? Was Lydia actually missing? And why? Outside of having known the Baron and the Bernard families for years, surely Lydia had no political activities.

Her arms aching to hold Caroline, Victoria resolutely tamped down her emotions. She had to think straight if she wanted to help.

She glanced over to where Dan was idly fingering one of Caroline's picture books. How could she begin to tell Dan about her suspicions that the baby's actual parentage was the reason Caroline had been taken? Only Lydia knew the truth. Whom had Lydia told? Such an admission would not only betray her marriage bargain with Rolande, it would cause an embarrassment to her country.

"Noticed anything missing?" Dan's question broke into Victoria's gloomy reverie.

"No, not yet. Actually," Victoria added, "I'm afraid I've been thinking instead of looking for clues."

She held a hand to her lips as she surveyed the empty crib. The rumpled bedclothes and the lingering sweet baby scent were an indication of the haste with which the baby had been taken.

She noticed that Caroline's favorite toy, a tiny chenille bear handmade by Lydia, was missing. It was a toy Lydia had lovingly embroidered with stars for eyes instead of using buttons, to protect Caroline from swallowing them.

She fought back tears as she noticed the hand-crocheted yellow afghan Lydia had made was also missing. The absence of these things gave her a small measure of comfort. In taking the things the baby loved, whoever had taken the baby had tried to make sure Caroline felt secure and safe.

"Lydia…" Horrified, she jumped to what she thought was a logical conclusion. She covered her lips with a shaking hand. Her father's betrayal tonight, that his country meant more to him than she did, had been bad enough, but now Lydia's! Had everyone she loved betrayed her?

Dan swung around at the sound. "What did you say?"

"Nothing," she murmured, unable to explain the unexplainable. A quick glance at Dan told her it might already be too late.

Dan strode to her side, turned her around and cupped her face in his hands. "Look at me! I'm on your side! So come out with it. I distinctly heard you say 'Lydia.' What about Lydia?"

Her mind in turmoil, Victoria gazed mutely at him. Could she trust him with her suspicions? And if she did tell him what she'd been thinking, would he realize he was Caroline's natural father?

"Come on, Victoria." His gaze seemed to soften as he gazed down at her. Instead of anger, she saw tenderness and an anxiety for her grow in his eyes. "I might not be the smartest guy around, but my hearing is damn good. You said something about Lydia. What was it?"

Victoria gazed at Dan and the frustration in eyes. He was right, she told herself. This was no time for games or half-truths.

After tonight, she mentally vowed, she was through trying to pretend that Rolande had been Caroline's father. Dan was the baby's father. She didn't know how much longer she could go on denying the truth to herself—or to him.

The miracle was that, in spite of her treatment of him, he was still at her side trying to help her find their daughter. What was the good of keeping her suspicions about Lydia and the kidnapping from him now?

She put her guilt at thinking Lydia was somehow involved aside. "It's only that I think that wherever Lydia has gone, she has taken Caroline with her."

Dan's eyes narrowed as he appeared to consider her statement. No wonder, she mused. She'd been praising Lydia to the skies only moments before, and now she was accusing her dearest friend of taking the baby!

"What makes you think so?"

"Because Caroline's favorite toy, a little yellow chenille stuffed bear, is missing." Victoria voice was almost breaking. "Also, the yellow afghan she likes so much is missing. Lydia made them both for Caroline."

"And that's enough to make you believe Lydia took the baby? A missing toy and a blanket?"

"That's enough for me to *think* she had something to do with it," she said, still unable to bring herself to believe Lydia would do such a thing. "No one else would have known about them or cared enough for the baby to have taken them."

Uncomfortable with his doubts, Dan studied the fear in Victoria's eyes, the unshed tears she struggled to hide.

"I guess Lydia could be the answer," he said as he'd surveyed the empty crib. "If you're sure, we'll start from there."

"I'm not sure. It's just something I feel inside."

"Maybe it's more than the baby's comfort Lydia was thinking about," Dan muttered. Surely a child's mother had to have a sixth sense about her baby.

He'd done his best, but he finally gave up trying to keep his distance from Victoria. At least for now, he didn't care if she had been another man's wife. She needed comfort and the contact of a sympathetic human being.

"Come here." Without stopping to worry about the consequences, he reached for her. "I need to hold you."

Her eyes darkened, her lips trembled. "I can't," she whispered.

"You can," he answered and took a step toward her. "Just for a little while."

Without a murmur she came into his arms. He pressed her to him and kissed the top of her head, murmuring soft words of reassurance. Now that she was in his arms again, it was all he'd needed to realize he knew the truth, he thought as he caressed her shoulders, the nape of her neck. For now, at least, this was where Victoria belonged—in his arms.

"Maybe Lydia taking the bear and the blanket was her way of sending you a message—all we have to do is to figure it out. At any rate, if she's involved in this, you don't have to worry. I'm sure she'll take good care of Caroline."

"Please, God," Victoria said as she leaned into

Dan's reassuring arms. "I hope and pray you're right and Caroline is safe."

"I'm sure she is," Dan assured her even though he knew Victoria's trust and belief in the people she cared for were at risk. Better to let her believe Lydia had left a message.

Dan quietly stroked the nape of Victoria's neck until he felt the muscles in her neck relax under his fingers. There was another way to ease Victoria's stress, his, too, he thought wryly. The bond he sensed growing between them would have to be satisfied sooner or later, but not until he found Caroline. The day when he could show his love for Victoria had to wait.

He took a deep breath. "Have you noticed anything else in the room missing?" he asked to distract himself from his thoughts.

"A diaper bag." Victoria sighed and moved out of his arms. "I always keep it filled with fresh diapers and dry formula. It didn't make any sense when I first noticed it was missing, but it does now."

Dan wished he had the same faith in Lydia that Victoria seemed to have. How could a woman so admired by the ambassador's household have taken the child who had been entrusted to her?

Unless Lydia was under some kind of threat of her own!

"Try to remember," he asked. "Can you think

of any reason why Lydia would voluntarily take the baby and disappear?''

Victoria bit her lower lip. ''Not voluntarily, no.'' How *could* she tell Dan about her suspicion that the kidnapping was planned ultimately to embarrass her family by threatening to reveal Caroline was illegitimate?

''Do you think Lydia wants the baby for herself?''

''No! Lydia isn't crazy. She loves Caroline.''

''All right,'' Dan replied. ''Let's take a look at Lydia's room. Maybe she's left a clue in there for us to find.''

Victoria was leading the way across the hall when her father strode into sight, stopping abruptly when he saw them. ''What are the two of you doing here? I have been waiting downstairs for you!''

To Dan's way of thinking, the man's anger wasn't because of his missing granddaughter. It was because Victoria hadn't obeyed him.

Basil Esterhazy actually put him in mind of the JAG, Admiral Crowley, a man whose bark was worse than his bite. Surely, at a time like this, Basil should have been more gentle with his daughter.

The conversation reminded him he hadn't gotten around to asking for a leave of absence. Damn! He glanced at his watch. No matter what time it was, he had to reach Crowley and get himself put on leave.

Even after the leave was granted, Dan knew he

was, contrary to his early assurances to Esterhazy, still a U.S. government employee. To make things worse, if he set one foot out of the embassy grounds, in or out of uniform, he was also Mike Wheeler's target as a prime suspect. Yet, true to his promise, until he got himself on leave, he had no right to remain here.

Except the right of a father to care for his child.

"We were just looking through your granddaughter's room for any clues as to her disappearance, sir," he said to deflect the ambassador's annoyance. "We were on our way downstairs," he added, with a warning glance Victoria. "I figured the nursery was the logical place to start."

When Victoria kept silent, it was obvious, at least to Dan, that she was reluctant to tell her father they had been about to search Lydia's room.

Basil frowned. "My staff has already looked in the nursery and found nothing missing."

Victoria broke into the conversation. "That's because they don't know what Caroline likes. Her favorite toy and blanket are missing."

"And this is important?"

"Yes, I think so," Victoria said to her father. "Let's go downstairs. Maybe someone in the room will remember something we all missed."

Dan hung back. Why didn't Victoria want her father to know she believed it was Lydia who had taken the baby and the missing items? It wasn't his right to question Victoria, but he'd be damned if he wasn't going to try to find some answers on his own.

First, he had to call Admiral Crowley. "If you don't mind, sir, why don't you go on ahead? I have to find a telephone and call my commanding officer to arrange for a short leave."

Obviously unused to having his orders thwarted, Esterhazy frowned. Dan held his gaze until the older man nodded his assent, but not before he saw a flicker of anger in the man's eyes.

The message in Victoria's eyes as she looked back at him was clear. She was asking Dan to come down to the library soon. He would, he vowed as he headed for a telephone that stood on a table at the end of the hall.

"YOU WANT to do what?" Crowley's voice thundered through the phone. Dan held it away to keep the noise from breaking an eardrum.

"I would like a two-week leave of absence, sir," Dan repeated after he expressed his regrets at the ungodly hour.

"Hell, no!" Crowley's voice grew louder. "You're not only disturbing my sleep, we're on overload at the office, or haven't you noticed?"

"I have, sir." Dan glanced around the hall to make sure he didn't have an audience. What he was about to tell the admiral wasn't for publication. "Something important has come up. I can't take care of it as long as I'm on duty, sir."

He heard Crowley swear before the man went on. "You're beginning to sound like Stevens. *He* needed time off to rescue his duchess and damned if he didn't wind up married her! You don't have a damsel in distress of your own, have you?"

"You might say that, sir."

"What in the hell does that mean? It better be good." Along with his obvious frustration, Crowley's voice grew louder.

"Off the record, sir, this damsel is only nine months old."

A stunned silence greeted him.

"If the leave isn't agreeable, sir," Dan went on before Crowley could speak, "I'd like to call in some of my considerable number of unused vacation days."

"Considerable!" Crowley's voice grew to a loud growl. "What in the hell is the difference between an unpaid leave and a vacation? And, let me tell you right now, there had damn well better be one."

"Vacations are mandated, sir," Dan replied respectfully. He decided to stick to the navy protocol Crowley understood. No way could he tell the admiral all about Caroline's kidnapping and the role he intended to play in her recovery. "The JAG medicos seem to believe vacations are necessary for a person's mental and physical health." He took a deep breath, mentally crossed his fingers and went on. "I haven't taken a vacation in two years."

"Well," Crowley answered, his voice slightly

softer but still obviously unhappy, "I'll put you down for two weeks. But you'd better get your butt back here when your time is up, or you'll hear from me!"

"Aye, aye, sir." Dan hung up, free at last to do what he would have done for Victoria anyway.

TWO DOZEN pairs of curious eyes greeted Dan when he finally walked into the library. A few members of the staff were in their night robes, some hadn't even bothered to undress. Several elderly members were nodding in their chairs at the rear of the room. Everyone looked unhappy at being ordered here at such an ungodly hour. Thank goodness, someone had taken the time to provide steaming pots of tea and coffee.

Victoria sat at her father's side, but her eyes lit up when Dan walked into the room.

"Good, you're finally here," the man said with a scowl. "Colonel Sandu was about to take a roll call to see who is missing from the embassy." He gestured to a tall, thin man with a goatee who stood in front of the desk. Although he was dressed in plain clothes, Dan easily recognized him as a member of the embassy's special forces.

From the dour looks of the man, Dan was sure Sandu and his men would probably have been the last persons to have befriended Lydia. Or to have looked twice at little Caroline. For damn sure, most of them hadn't been on board long enough to have recognized that a stuffed bear or an afghan were missing from the baby's crib.

Dan nodded briefly to the ambassador, poured himself a cup of black coffee and sauntered to the back of the room where he could observe the proceedings. The roll call might tell him who was missing besides Lydia, but he had a gut feeling the count wouldn't reveal the identity of the real culprit. Or the culprit's accomplice.

To Dan's way of thinking, Sandu and his staff should already have had a history or profile of everyone on the embassy staff. It was the only way to determine the likelihood of anyone either falling under the influence of the kidnapper or of being the kidnapper himself.

He glanced around the room. The only person he could identify was the chauffeur Victoria had mentioned. He recognized Stefan because the driver was still in uniform.

Victoria was sitting quietly beside her father, her hands folded in her lap. The picture of a good and dutiful daughter, but from the way she sat there with that grim look on her face, it didn't look to him as if she was satisfied with Sandu's routine. Or that she was about to share her suspicions this morning. Not with her father, anyway.

He sipped his coffee to distract himself, but inside he was seething. Contrary to vows he'd made to himself to distance himself from Victoria, he was more disturbed at the role she played tonight than he should be. As far as he'd already learned, Victoria was an intelligent and strong woman, not the robot who sat so silently, so defeated. What was the role she played as the ambassador's daughter doing to her sweet disposition, her natural exuberance?

Was he the only one who sensed the anguish that was tearing her apart?

His attention was drawn to the list of employees the colonel was reading. Thank goodness it was short.

True to Dan's prediction, Lydia wasn't the only person missing. "Fritz is also missing tonight," Sandu finally added as he put the list in his pocket. "Considering his injuries, however, he couldn't have played a part in taking Caroline." He bowed to the ambassador. "We shall be ready to resume our search in the morning, sir. Will that be all for tonight?"

Dan wanted to shout that the roll call wasn't all that was needed tonight. By any rational thought, Sandu should have had his men spread out on the embassy property searching for footprints or fingerprints. If they waited, physical clues could be trampled over or removed by someone who knew the culprits.

"To bed, everyone," Esterhazy announced and glanced at his watch. "We will have breakfast at 6:00 a.m. We will resume the search in daylight at 6:30."

The staff slowly drifted away. Esterhazy glanced

at Dan. ''There are a few hours before we can resume our search of the embassy grounds, Mr.
O'Hara. If you like, a room will be made ready for
you.''

Dan nodded and smiled grimly. Sleep was the last
thing on his mind, but he could scarcely prowl the
embassy by himself. Or, heaven forbid, be found
checking Lydia's room.

A sleepy maid directed him to a room in the family quarters before she bobbed a curtsy and ran down
the servants' stairs.

Exhausted, Dan fought to keep his eyes open. He
started to shuck off his clothing to grab a few moments' rest and was down to his boxers when he
froze. He slept in the nude at home, only this wasn't
his home.

After due consideration, he left on his boxers, slid
into bed and waited for exhaustion to overtake him.
It wasn't working. Ten minutes ago he hadn't been
able to keep his eyes open. Now he couldn't sleep.

Maybe it was the idea of sleeping with Victoria
only yards away that made his body stir and kept
his mind busy. It sure couldn't have been the unfamiliar surroundings—he'd slept in hundreds of unfamiliar rooms all over the world, some of which he
was more than happy to forget. This one, at least,
was a luxurious bedroom with its own adjoining
bathroom.

Maybe, he finally decided, it was the uneasy feeling of having left a job undone that kept him awake.

He'd wait until everyone was asleep before he made his next move.

First, he had to sort out his thoughts about Caroline's mother.

After he'd unexpectedly met Victoria again, it hadn't taken him long to realize there was more than a sexual attraction between them. If their earlier encounter had only been a one-night stand, the way he felt about her wouldn't have lasted all this time. It ran deeper than that. Instead of the bond he sensed between them being only an ordinary man-woman attraction, he wanted Victoria as deeply as a man wants the woman he loves—a woman he wants to spend the rest of his life with.

VICTORIA quietly accepted her father's good-night kiss on her cheek and went into her room. She'd interpreted Dan's glance as a silent request that she meet him later to help him check Lydia's room. She would have to do it after she made sure everyone was asleep. There was no way she would be able to explain her and Dan being together again.

An hour later, with a small flashlight she kept for emergencies in her hand, she cautiously opened the door to Lydia's room. If Lydia had intended to stay away for any length of time, there was no sign of it. Her suitcases were in the corner of the closet and everything was neatly in its place. Whatever had happened to take Lydia away from the embassy had to have been a last-minute decision.

A movement at the door startled her. She darted behind a folding screen when the door opened and, to her relief, Dan O'Hara slipped inside the room.

Dan put his finger to his lips. "Sorry, I couldn't sleep. I didn't know you'd be in here."

"Oh, I'm so glad it's only you!" she whispered. She threw herself into his arms as if they'd hadn't parted only moments ago. "I was afraid it could be a member of the embassy's security forces."

"They're probably all asleep waiting for the sun to shine," he said wryly as he rubbed her cold hand between his own. "Better now?"

"Yes." Looking guilty, she pulled away. "I don't even know what I'm supposed to be looking for in here! Lydia is always so neat and everything looks so normal."

At Victoria's comment, Dan gazed around the room. She was right. The bed, with its ruffled pillows, had clearly not been slept in. A book and Lydia's reading glasses waited on the nightstand. A pair of slippers was neatly lined up beside the bed.

"Maybe that's the clue we've been waiting for," he said softly as he knelt and looked under the bed. "I've been around women enough to know that women never travel without some luggage. I also know that the first thing they pick up when they leave in a hurry is their handbag. Where's Lydia's?"

"There." She pointed to a large carpetbag. "Over on the dresser."

"Let's take a look inside."

Victoria emptied the contents of the purse on the bedspread and shone the flashlight on it. "It looks as if everything she uses every day is here."

"Then I'm sure she intended to come right back."

"You really think so?" Victoria looked doubtful as she pored over the contents of the purse.

"Put yourself in Lydia's place," Dan said and pointed to the bed. "Would you leave your purse, your lipstick and your money behind if you were going to be away from home for any length of time?"

"Then you think whatever happened had to have happened suddenly…?"

"And with someone Lydia knew…" Dan added. He checked the empty bathroom adjoining Lydia's room. "…or the room would have looked as if she'd put up a fight."

In the dim light of the flashlight, Victoria seemed to blanch at the thought. "What do we do now?"

"One thing is damn sure, Lydia didn't pack for a long stay," Dan replied as he gazed at the neatly stacked suitcases. "She's probably with someone who hadn't expected to take her along when he took Caroline. My theory is that Lydia surprised him."

At the growing look of anguish on Victoria's face, he took her in his arms and held her until she stopped shivering. "Don't worry, I have a feeling that Lydia and Caroline can't be too far away."

As he held Victoria and tried to reassure her, a

vision of Lydia and Caroline riding in the rear seat of an embassy limousine flashed through his mind. Driving off the embassy grounds would have been easy. The car wouldn't have been stopped—not if the driver was known to be an embassy chauffeur!

But Stefan, the current chauffeur, had been in the library earlier! There was only one person who could have driven Lydia and Caroline away without comment.

"Dan? Have you thought of something?" Victoria glanced up at him. "You look so grim."

He couldn't tell her what he'd been thinking—not until he had some kind of proof. Right now, he had to remember it was Victoria who needed him.

Before he could stop to remember he had no right to show Victoria how much he cared for her, he pressed her to his chest, kissed her forehead, the corners of each of her eyes and her cheeks. He had to have more, but not without her consent. "Victoria?"

"Not enough," he heard her murmur as she clung to him. "It's been so long since…"

Dan felt the pounding of her heart and recognized her frustration. A frustration that mirrored his own. He didn't want to stop to ask her what she meant by that half-whispered remark—*it's been so long…* It was enough to think she wanted him as much as he wanted her.

"Victoria, I…" he said, afraid he was about to

take advantage of her vulnerability. ''…are you sure about this?''

She dropped the flashlight onto the bed and raised her lips to his for his kiss. Her breasts rose and fell against his chest as her desire, coupled with her need for comfort, overwhelmed her. So good… Dan thought for a brief moment as shocks of heat enveloped him. He was happy he was the man that Victoria had turned to in her time of need.

Dan forgot his vow to get out of Victoria's life. From the way she clung to him, and from the way he sensed she needed the comfort of his arms and his reassurance, he was a goner.

He couldn't hold back. Not when he'd been dreaming of Victoria, wanting her, needing her, just as she seemed to need him. He had to believe she truly cared for him, that her frantic need to be held in his arms tonight wasn't just an attempt to escape from reality into the world she'd created for herself.

Chapter Twelve

Victoria felt as if she was floating on air when Dan claimed her lips in a deep and passionate kiss. Time stood still, the room they were in faded. It was if some time warp had taken her back to the magical hours in Baronovia when she'd first met Dan O'Hara and spent the night in his arms.

Never before and never since, she thought wistfully as she burrowed deeper into his arms, had she felt such a physical attraction to a man as she had to Dan that night and now.

Her heart raced until she was afraid she wouldn't be able to breathe, warmth flushed over her body. Instinctively her arms came up around his neck to bring him closer, and closer still. She felt his hard body press into hers. He was as aroused as she was. He murmured her name and slid his hands over her shoulders, pausing at her breasts then moving down to her waist. She thought she would dissolve in a ball of fire. Desire, long buried within her, surfaced.

This was the only man she'd ever made love with, she thought as he deepened his kiss. And the only man she would ever love.

Heaven help her, she longed to make passionate love with Dan again. To know the scent of him, the taste of him, to have him fill the ache within her. To make her feel alive.

Denied by circumstance of the physical loving she'd yearned for since that night long ago, she'd gone through the charade of a real marriage with Rolande. Although her husband had sometimes held her in silent understanding, she had never been able to forget the burst of pleasure when Dan had made her his. To have known that pleasure only once surely had to have been her punishment for keeping the truth from Dan.

If fate hadn't intervened back in Baronovia, she would have sought him out, for he was the man she'd believed was her destiny. Instead, at her father's insistence, a month later she'd not only been engaged to marry Rolande Bernard, she'd discovered she was pregnant. Even though Rolande had known he was impotent, he had still been eager for the marriage. His impotence had almost been a blessing. The automobile accident that had taken him from her had broken her heart. Rumors that the accident had been planned by Baronovian dissidents still hung in the air. Another reason to fear for Caroline's safe return.

She knew she had no right to complain. Rolande

had been a good friend to her and a loving father to Caroline. Tonight she had suffered heartbreak again when she'd discovered her baby's disappearance. Brokenly, she clung to Dan.

Abruptly, Dan drew back from their kiss. He crushed her against him for a moment, then held her away from him again. Surprised at the break in his embrace, she was shattered by the fleeting look of regret she saw pass over his eyes.

"I'm sorry, sweetheart," he said as he took a deep breath, "I shouldn't have done that. I have no right to. Not now, anyway."

Victoria was bewildered. A moment ago, she'd felt the wild beating of his heart. Now, instead of sharing the embrace that brought back so many wonderful memories, there was something different about him. As quickly as her spirits had risen, they fell.

How could she have been mistaken about the way Dan felt about her? "Is something wrong?"

"No, something is very right," he said ruefully as he gently rubbed his hands over her back. "I'm just not sure what it is..." His voice faded off. "I guess I finally realized what you meant a moment ago. I know I don't have the right to ask, but when you said 'it's been so long...' did you mean you and Bernard never..." He paused, as if unable to continue. "Have I read you right?"

"Not since you," she said softly, afraid she would lose Dan again, this time for good. She was a widow with a child. Would he believe he had been her only lover? And, even if he did, what possible good could come of it? "I know you'll find it hard to believe, but it's true."

"But you were married to Bernard." He paused and bit his lower lip as if debating how to say it. "Are you saying I was the only man who..."

"...who made love to me? Yes, you are my only lover," she said, schooling herself not to weep. "I hadn't ever meant to tell you, but so much has happened here tonight I hardly know what I'm doing or saying."

"But you had a husband?"

"I know. Rolande was happy to make me his wife, even in name only. To his sorrow, he was impotent—it is a secret that was known only to the two of us. He was eager to marry me because he wanted to be able to show the world he had fathered a child."

Obviously shocked, Dan gazed down at her. "My God, I was right! I'm Caroline's father?"

"Yes," she said, gazing into his eyes, the same shape and color as her baby's eyes. "I thought you'd already guessed."

"I was pretty sure, but I didn't want to push you." He crushed her to his chest again and smoothed her hair away from her forehead. "Imagine that, I'm a father!" he said softly.

"Are you sorry?" she said anxiously, searching

his face for the truth. "Don't be. I'll never ask you for anything."

"Sorry?" Dan remembered when he'd been left without parents long ago. Remembered his loneliness and unhappiness until his uncle adopted him a year later.

"No," he went on with a smile. "I'm very pleased. I like kids. It's just that I hadn't gotten around to thinking seriously about a family." He debated telling Victoria about his five-year plan, but suddenly the plan turned to sawdust in his mind. What would a family be without Victoria as his wife?

"But you, Victoria," he went on, deeply saddened at the thought of what she must have gone through since that night in Baronovia, "I'm so sorry I was never there for you when you needed me."

"I was going to look for you the next morning, but my father told me he'd already planned my marriage to Rolande. After I found I was pregnant, for the sake of my unborn child, I felt I had no choice. I will always be grateful to Rolande for giving me and Caroline a safe and secure future," she said, her voice breaking. "And now someone has taken her from me. Oh, Dan, she's such a sweet baby, and now she's gone!"

"Not for long," Dan swore under his breath. "I intend to find Caroline for you, but there's one thing I need to ask. Bernard. Was he good to you?"

"Yes. And all this time I thought that I should be

faithful to his memory…but now I don't know anymore. I do know that he loved me as much as he was able to. I also know he would be happy for me, now that I've met you again. But—'' she hesitated ''—Caroline must remain his child. I owe him that much.''

A sad smile came over Dan's face. He smiled and ran a gentle finger over her chin.

''The most important thing right now is to get Caroline back,'' he said with a wry smile. ''That's the reason why I asked for a leave of absence. I wanted to be a free man so I could look for Caroline without any rules and regulations to stop me.''

Victoria swallowed a reply. Surely, she thought, Dan must have realized by now that he was being put to the test. The test of finding his own child.

She took a deep breath and pulled out of Dan's arms. ''I should apologize for coming to you like this,'' she said. ''I'm afraid I couldn't help myself.''

''No apology necessary.'' He gently stroked her chin. ''If you hadn't gotten carried away, sweetheart, I would have.''

In spite of Dan's reassurance, Victoria knew the intimate moments between them were over. The terrible reality of her missing daughter came over her. ''What do we do now?''

''We find the baby.''

''How, where?'' She gazed frantically around the empty room. ''Have I missed something?''

''Maybe,'' he said and picked up the flashlight.

"I'm not sure yet, but I think I have a pretty good idea of what to do next. Come on, it's almost six-thirty. Let's go downstairs and join the others."

A SMALL GROUP of the embassy staff had already gathered when Dan and Victoria arrived in the embassy's kitchen. Gleaming pots and pans hung over the huge stove. A cook was grimly flipping pancakes. Dan's stomach growled, but he had more important things on his mind than breakfast.

Colonel Sandu glanced up from his position at the head of the staff table. There was a heaping plate of pancakes in front of the security officer. This morning he was in uniform, as if to remind Dan of his position within the embassy. Dan wasn't impressed. "Ah, Mr. O'Hara. I was hoping to speak to you this morning," he sneered. "That is, if you were still with us."

Dan nodded curtly and pulled out a chair for Victoria. If Sandu thought insults were the way to get rid of him, the man had another think coming. "Good, because you're just the man I wanted to speak to myself. You first," he added, ignoring the brief flash of anger in Sandu's eyes. As far as he could tell, Sandu had red tape running in his veins instead of blood.

"I understand you are a commander in the United States Navy?"

"I'm an officer in the Navy Department's Judge

Advocate General's Corps," Dan agreed. "At the moment I'm on leave. Why?"

"We are concerned that this matter remain within these walls, Commander," Sandu said suavely. "And I am curious about your interest in this case."

"The ambassador has my word on that matter," Dan said shortly. "As to my interest, let's just say I'm a friend of Mrs. Bernard's. Now, if you don't mind, I have a question for you. Is Stefan, the chauffeur, a member of the embassy's special forces?"

Sandu glanced at Victoria, as if to question Dan's right to ask questions.

She gave him an even look. "Go on, Colonel Sandu. Answer Mr. O'Hara's question."

Sandu shrugged. "Yes."

"And Fritz?"

"No, he is not."

Dan realized Sandu was angry as hell and that he wasn't going to get a lot of information out of him, but he persisted. "Have you asked the chauffeur, Fritz, about his whereabouts last night?"

"The man is in a cast from his injuries," Sandu scoffed. "There was no point in disturbing him."

Sandu's narrowed eyes gave away his frustration, but Dan didn't care. Invalid or not, Fritz was going to get a visitor before the day was through.

To make matters worse, as far as Dan was concerned, Sandu was doing a lousy job as a crime investigator. He locked his eyes with the colonel's, until Sandu's eyes slid away. "Where was Stefan at the time of the kidnapping?"

The colonel hesitated. "He was assisting arriving guests."

"And incidentally screening them for admittance?"

Sandu nodded. "We went over all this last night, Commander, when you returned for the second time from your so-called errand. What are you suggesting?"

Dan didn't like the sarcastic way the man used the word *errand,* but he wasn't going to let the man stop him from asking questions. "Just that I believe the guests probably didn't have anything to do with the kidnapping. I believe that the kidnapper was someone everyone here knew. Someone who was able to take advantage of all the activity last night without worrying about the probability of being questioned."

A stunned silence fell over the kitchen. Dan ambled over to the service island and poured himself a cup of coffee from a giant chrome coffee urn. Ignoring the platters of still-warm scrambled eggs and sliced bacon, he turned away. "Unless you want to stay for breakfast—" he glanced at Victoria "—I'd like to speak to you in the library."

She shook her head. "I'm not hungry. All this talking. We have to find my baby!"

"We will, I promise." Dan shot Sandu a cold look. "Go on with your breakfast, Colonel. Mrs.

Bernard and I have some talking to do. If you should need us, you'll find us in the library.''

Victoria led the way to the library and sank into a large leather chair. ''What now?''

Dan hung back and deliberately leaned against the closed door instead of taking her in his arms as he wanted to. ''Victoria, there's a lot I want to say to you, but not just yet. Caroline comes first. Right now, I'd like you to tell me everything you know about your chauffeur Fritz.''

''I've already told you Fritz is not only Lydia's nephew, he's my friend.''

Dan's heart ached at the desolate look that came over Victoria's face at the possibility Fritz had taken Caroline. And that her dear Lydia had gone with him. She may have told him she was content with her life, but she must have been lonely or her chauffeur wouldn't have managed to become her friend.

It was beginning to look as if Victoria had been betrayed by all the people she trusted the most. First, her father, then Lydia and now Fritz. But she still had him.

He moved away from the door, careful to keep his distance from Victoria. He wanted to comfort her, to hold her in his arms and make love to her until he brought a smile back into her exquisite eyes. It wasn't fair that she had to have been his for only that one night in Baronovia, he told himself bitterly.

He sat down behind the carved desk to keep a distance between himself and Victoria. By involving her in his search for her daughter, he would be able to keep her from dwelling on the worst scenario.

"Tell me more about Fritz, please. Who are his friends? Where does he go when he's not on duty?"

"I know Fritz has some friends who live in Georgetown. I remember he told me they're exchange students at the Georgetown University. I know that at least one of them has an apartment near the university. Fritz goes there to wait for me when I'm out shopping or when he has free time."

Dan pounced on her answer. "Exchange students from Baronovia?"

"I'm sorry. I didn't ask and I don't think Fritz ever mentioned their nationality. I once asked Fritz why he didn't go to the university here himself, but I never got an answer."

Dan felt too close to an eye-opening discovery to give up. "Is it possible there was still some lingering discontent among nationalists and students over Baronovia's diplomatic affiliation with the United States?"

Victoria stopped to think, her face blanched. "The same discontent that got my cousin May involved in demonstrations here in Washington?"

"Yep. If Fritz hangs around foreign exchange students from Baronovia, maybe he got himself caught up in some leftover nationalist fever."

"Not with his Aunt Lydia's knowledge," Victoria protested. "Lydia wouldn't let him become one of them. She's not only devoted to Caroline, she's been a friend of our family for years.''

''She might not have known. Tell me, how does Fritz feel about the exchange of ambassadors between Baronovia and the United States?''

This time Victoria didn't even have to stop to think. ''Why? I told you Fritz and I are friends! We've never discussed politics.''

''Maybe,'' Dan agreed as he rubbed his forehead. ''With all the free time he evidently has on his hands, he's young enough to be impressionable. Maybe even to become influenced by some fanatic students from your homeland.''

Victoria's eyes widened. She started to protest, then stopped. ''What does that have to do with my baby?''

Dan hated himself for frightening her, but he couldn't let go of the gut feeling he was on to something. ''Maybe nothing, but right now it's the only lead I have. It looks as if Fritz is the only one who has free entry to and from the embassy. He's also the only staff member who wasn't here last night and early this morning.''

''Why would he take Caroline?''

Dan wandered around the library. He picked up the framed Bernard family photograph and studied it for a moment before he put it back on the desk. ''To have something to hold over your family,'' he said thoughtfully. ''Taking Caroline was probably the only way the people Fritz was working with could get your father's attention.''

Panic seized Victoria. She started for the door. ''Oh, my God! Do you suppose… Could Fritz have somehow learned that Rolande wasn't Caroline's father and told his friends? I have to talk to my father and tell him of your suspicions! I shouldn't have waited this long!''

Dan grabbed her arm before she could leave. ''Who *does* know the truth about Caroline?''

''Lydia, May and now you!'' Victoria said as she tried to pull away. ''Lydia would never have told Fritz! Never! She loves the baby as much as I do!''

''I think she did tell Fritz,'' Dan said, ''and we still don't know what Fritz intends to do. He may have taken the baby himself for ransom money. When Lydia found out, she could have gone along to protect Caroline. One way or another, I'm sure we'll probably hear soon.''

Just then Basil Esterhazy strode into the room waving a white envelope. ''It's here, just as I suspected! A ransom note has just been delivered by special messenger!''

''Is Caroline all right? Are they asking for money?'' Victoria rushed to her father and reached for the ransom note.

''Apparently she is, and no,'' Esterhazy bit out as he handed the note to her, ''it appears that whoever they are, they're not interested in money.''

''Pardon me, sir,'' Dan asked, hanging back out

of courtesy, "who do they say they are? What *are* they asking for?"

"They sign themselves the Faithful. The fools demand Victoria resign as ambassador and go home to Baronovia. They also demand we close the embassy and sever all diplomatic ties with the United States!"

"Fat chance, sir," Dan said dryly. "They haven't a prayer. Don't they realize the choice to close the embassy isn't Victoria's to make? That the ruler of your country and my own State Department will have something to say about it once we tell them about the note?"

"The note remains private," the ambassador warned. "Colonel Sandu will handle it."

"Pardon me, sir, but Sandu couldn't find his way out of an open door. I'm willing to bet I know who the culprits are. Give me a couple of hours, and I'll have Rolande's daughter back home."

While he waited for Esterhazy's, as Victoria's chargé d'affaires, permission to move ahead, Dan's heart grew heavy at the sacrifice he'd just made. Victoria might think he'd relinquished his claim to their baby but he hadn't. All he had actually done, if the truth about Caroline's father ever came out, was to give Victoria's father the signal that he would keep quiet about his relationship to Caroline. It was the least he could do. Esterhazy was, after all, Victoria's father and Caroline's grandfather.

"My baby!" Victoria cried as she studied the ransom note through tear-filled eyes. "We have to find her!"

Dan reluctantly stepped aside as Esterhazy put a consoling arm around Victoria. "We will find Caroline, my dear. Why don't you go to your room and try to get some rest while I discuss the ransom note with Colonel Sandu?"

Dan bit back a remark; the ambassador hadn't bought his offer. To hell with it! The ambassador could discuss the note with the colonel until kingdom come, but in the meantime the trail was growing cold. And, at the rate the embassy's special forces were moving, it would grow even colder. He motioned to Victoria and gave a slight nod of his head toward the door.

Victoria pulled out of her father's embrace. "Yes, of course, father. You will call me when you decide what to do? I need to know."

Before her father agreed, Dan could sense the great effort it took for Victoria to look as if she was reacting calmly to her father's request. What kind of man was Esterhazy not to see the frantic look in Victoria's eyes? Why was he sending her away when it was obvious it was important to her to stay and help find her daughter?

"I shall look in on you soon, and tell you of any progress, my dear," Esterhazy said as he nodded to Dan and left the library.

Victoria waited until her father was out of sight before she turned to Dan. "You have something in mind, don't you? And before *you* suggest I go upstairs and rest, the answer is no! Whatever you do, or wherever you go, I'm going with you.''

''I wouldn't have it any other way,'' Dan replied with rueful acceptance. ''You have more guts and brains packed in your beautiful body than a dozen Colonel Sandus. And you're a hell of a lot prettier, too,'' he added with a grin.

He couldn't help himself. Levity at a time like this was nothing short of ridiculous, but he had to do something to ease the anguish he saw in Victoria's eyes.

Happily, he watched her blush. ''Go on, what are you planning?'' she said.

''I intended to speak to Stefan, your current chauffeur. Since the man is a member of the embassy special forces and appears to be sharper than his superior, I thought he should be in the loop. But now that the ransom note is here, I don't have the time. So it boils down to this,'' he said as he paced the floor. ''We're going to have to find Fritz by ourselves.''

''I don't understand. How will you know where to find him?''

''That's where you come in.'' He wanted to call Victoria sweetheart again, but once had been enough. Enough to make him realize he was rapidly moving from being her former lover to a man who was falling head over heels with her. Burdening her with the confession of his love wouldn't be fair to her.

Keep her busy, he told himself. Keep her too busy to see you make a fool out of yourself. "Did you actually see the crash that sidelined Fritz?"

"No. After the accident, I went up to his room above the garages to bring him some fruit and cookies."

"He was there?"

"Yes. He was in bed covered by a blanket, but he told me his foot was in a cast. I did see his arm, though," she said thoughtfully. "It was in a sling."

"A sling. Not a cast?"

"No, I don't think so."

"I'm going to call the garage apartment in a minute," Dan said as he looked out the window at the first rays of sunshine, "but I'm willing to bet that Fritz wasn't seriously injured and that he's not up there. I think the automobile accident was part of a plot that, willingly or not, he found himself involved in. I'm even ready to bet he's with his friends in Georgetown right now, and that, when we find them, we'll find Lydia and Caroline."

Dan used the intercom to call the garage apartment. When no one answered, he turned back to Victoria. "He's not there. I'm sure he was faking those injuries. Do you think you could find the apartment in Georgetown that Fritz visits?"

"No. I was only there once. I waited in the car while Fritz went upstairs to pick up something he'd forgotten." She paused. "Wait a minute! I saw

Lydia's address book among the contents of her purse. It may have the address we're looking for!''

Dan watched admiringly as Victoria's face lit up, and she disappeared through the door. He had been right to involve her in the search for Caroline—not that he would have been able to stop her. From the old-fashioned, docile woman she'd seemed to be, she'd turned into a proactive twenty-first-century modern woman. He didn't know how her family was going to take the change in her, but he liked it just fine.

Chapter Thirteen

His mind seething with the prospect of finding Fritz, Dan anxiously prowled the library. The last thing he needed was to have Colonel Sandu show up before Victoria came downstairs with Lydia's address book.

He knew damn well the colonel would mount a conference to debate the pros and cons of looking for Fritz before he took any action. Hell, the man didn't even seem to want to believe that Fritz *could* be involved in the kidnapping! Didn't the guy realize that the longer he waited to find Fritz, the farther away the baby could be taken?

"I have the book!" Victoria whispered as she rushed into the library. "I was right. There *is* a Georgetown address and telephone number listed for Fritz!"

"Did anyone see you?" Dan reached for the small black book and opened it to the page with Fritz's name on it. To his surprise it was splashed with tearstains. If Dan needed any further proof that Lydia was somehow involved in the kidnapping, the stains confirmed it. It looked as if Lydia had cried over her nephew more than once.

"I don't think so. Since everyone is in the kitchen, I used the servants' stairs." Victoria caught her breath and craned her neck to look at the open address book. "What do we do now?"

"We find a car," Dan said, plowing his fingers through his hair. "I don't dare use mine. Sandu and company have probably staked it out by now."

Even as he spoke, Dan heard the faint sound of voices coming down the hall. He hurriedly stuffed the little black book into his pocket. "There have to be a dozen cars in the embassy garage," he said with a frustrated glance out the window. "I have to get my hands on some wheels before company arrives!"

"No problem." Victoria felt in the pocket of her slacks and drew out a key. "I knew you would want this sooner or later."

Dan stared at Victoria's sparkling green eyes. As an accomplice, she was priceless. As a woman, she was driving him to distraction. It wasn't easy keeping his mind on automobiles when she looked so pleased with herself. Whoever thought brains and beauty didn't mix hadn't met Victoria.

"Your own car? I thought Fritz took you everywhere." Dan fought off the sinking sensation he was losing a battle with himself. He might have the best of intentions, but he was damned if he knew how he was going to be able to walk away from Victoria once Caroline was rescued.

"It was my birthday present to myself, but my father insisted I always have a bodyguard with me when I used it. Somehow it was easier to let Fritz take me wherever I wanted to go."

"Thanks." Dan considered what Victoria had just given away—she felt trapped in her present situation. He shoved the key in his pocket and looked around for an unguarded exit. He would have stopped to show Victoria his gratitude, but it was only a matter of time before Sandu showed up. "I'm going to Georgetown to get the SOB who took Caroline. You wait here. I'll be back as soon as I can."

"You mean *we're* going to Georgetown," Victoria said firmly and started after him. She shrugged into the jacket she carried. "Let's go."

His hand on the nearest French door, Dan glanced over his shoulder. "You can't come with me. There's no telling what might happen."

"I don't care," Victoria said firmly. "Fritz wouldn't hurt me. We are friends."

"Yeah, some friend," Dan muttered. He opened a French door, glanced outside to make sure no one was nearby, and pulled Victoria after him. To his relief, the coast to the garage was clear. When they got there, a dozen cars were neatly lined up. "Which one is yours?"

Victoria pointed to a dark-green Lexus. The exterior had been polished to a high sheen, the windshield sparkled and even the four tires glistened.

"Good. Since I know D.C. better than you do, I'll do the driving. Let's hope there's gas in the tank."

"Fritz prides himself on keeping all the cars gassed and ready to go." Victoria studied the row of cars and frowned. "You were right, the embassy limousine is missing!"

"I knew it!" Dan opened the car door for Victoria and strode around the other side. "Fritz must have put on his chauffeur's uniform last night and used the limo to get away. Smart move," he said ruefully as he backed out of the garage, "with dozens of limos and their drivers around, he banked on no one trying to stop him."

Dan clenched his teeth when he saw a flash of fear cross Victoria's eyes. He reached over and put a free hand on her knee. She put her left hand over his and smiled her gratitude. "Everything is going to turn out just fine," he said before he turned his attention to getting off the embassy grounds without being stopped.

Dan released the brake and slowly backed the car out of the garage. As he approached the embassy gates, he heard someone shout for him to stop.

"Make sure your seat belt is fastened and hang on," he said to Victoria as he gunned the car and took off. A few blocks later, he slowed the car and turned into a fast-food parking lot full of cars where they wouldn't be noticed. "Take a look at the address book and read me the entry she has for Fritz."

"93 Volta Place." Victoria looked out the window. "I remember the street is somewhere near the university. I just don't remember how to get there."

"No problem," Dan said grimly. He punched the address into the GPS system on the dashboard. "There, just off the university, near the Convent of the Visitation!"

As Dan set the car in motion, Victoria prayed silently for her baby daughter's safety. Her rational mind told her Lydia had gone with her nephew. Lydia would take care of Caroline. At the same time, her heart ached to feel those tiny fingers curl around hers. To see that sunny little dimpled smile again, the four new little teeth.

As if he knew what she was thinking, Dan put his hand back on her knee. "We'll have Caroline back soon, I promise."

Victoria put her own hand over Dan's for a moment. Not only to thank him for his reassurance, but to feel the touch of a caring hand. Even though they'd met only a few times since their encounter in Baronovia, he was the man she was in love with. Maybe, her heart told her, Dan needed her touch as much as she needed his.

Dan found a parking spot a block away from the Volta Place address. "Do you want to wait here while I look around?

"No. I'm going with you." Victoria drew away

and reached for the car door. How could she sit quietly and let Dan go into possible danger when she had as much at stake as he did?

Dan shrugged helplessly. "I don't know why I even asked. Come on."

93 Volta Place turned out to be an ancient four-family apartment house. Weathered wooden siding and faded layers of paint covered the outside. Worn lace curtains covered upstairs windows. The bottom windows were covered with sagging shutters.

Dan stood in front of the bank of mailboxes, none of which carried Fritz's name. "We could gamble," he muttered as he studied the boxes, "but my guess is that we're looking for one of the ground-floor apartments. If Fritz's buddies are up to no good, they would choose a downstairs apartment for a quick getaway. Ready?"

Her heart pumping in her chest, Victoria eyed the mailboxes and nodded. "How are you going to get inside?"

"Like this." Dan punched the doorbell beneath each of the first two mailboxes and waited expectantly. Instead of a buzzer that opened the door, a shuttered window opened.

"Who are you and what do you want?" an elderly woman asked.

"Sorry, I must have punched the wrong doorbell," Dan apologized. "We're from the INS," he said, improvising as he went along. "We're looking for a couple of foreign exchange students who have overstayed their visas.''

He was taking a chance and he knew it, but after seeing the annoyed look on the woman's face, he sensed it wouldn't take much for her to vent her frustration.

''Humph,'' she said, with a glance at Victoria. ''Those two men spend their time hanging around the place. Unsavory visitors coming and going all night. Never saw them carry a book, either. If they're actually students, I'd be surprised. Are you going to deport them?''

''Not without a hearing,'' Dan told her, in case she was a law-minded citizen. ''Do you happen to know where they are right now?''

''They left early this morning in a limousine…woke me up, by the way,'' she said with a dark look. ''When you find them, tell them they might as well pack up and go home. If they stay, I'm going to evict them for disturbing the peace and for nonpayment of rent.''

''You're the landlady?''

''Been one for thirty years,'' she said as she reached to close the shutters, ''and never had any tenants like those two before.''

''Excuse me,'' Victoria said before the shutters closed, ''could we go inside their apartment and look around?''

''I guess so,'' she grumbled. ''It's a furnished apartment, and the rental agreement says I have the right to make sure nothing is stolen. I'll buzz you in. Just make sure you don't take anything without telling me!''

"Yes, ma'am." Dan would have agreed to anything to get inside the apartment and check for clues. "We won't be long."

"What next?" Victoria looked troubled as she followed him inside the apartment. "Just what *are* we looking for?''

"Something that will show us what our friends are doing here. According to their landlady, it isn't studying at the university.''

Inside the apartment, Dan quickly located a computer, a color copier and stacks of newly printed handbills.

"What are those?" Victoria asked nervously.

"They're sure not homework," Dan answered as he shuffled through the printed papers. "Seems they want the U.S. out of the affairs of small European countries, namely Baronovia.''

"Did you find any signs of Fritz?"

"No, but I'll bet he's one of those unsavory characters the landlady talked about.''

Victoria shuddered. "What are we going to do now?"

Good intentions be damned, Dan thought as he dropped the handbills back into a cardboard box. The unhappiness he saw on Victoria's face hit him where it hurt—in his heart. If anyone needed the warmth of reassuring human touch right now, it was she. He took a deep breath and reached for her.

"I may hate myself for this later, Victoria," he said softly, "but right now I need to hold you."

Victoria didn't hesitate. "That's good," she said with a shy smile as she went into Dan's arms, "because I need you to hold me." The look on his face as he lowered his lips to hers wasn't sympathetic or compassionate. It was the look of a man in love with a woman. She felt herself warm as she melted into his arms.

"Don't talk anymore," she murmured. "If you care for me, show me."

He held her face between his hands and gazed into her eyes. "Care for you? More than I should," he whispered as he caressed her lips with his own. To her delight, he went on to caress the nape of her neck and the hollow between her breasts. His hands slid over her shoulders and down to her waist before he stopped.

"This *has* to be the wrong time and the wrong place," he said between short, hard gasps. "And I have to be the wrong man."

"The right man, the only man," she whispered. "If only I had waited to find you again."

"There was the baby," he answered. "I blame myself for that, too."

"You mustn't. I've already told you how happy I am to have Caroline. And to have had you."

He kissed her again.

Victoria clung to Dan when she was able to come up for air. Regardless of what tomorrow might bring, at least she had these moments to remember. Just as she had never forgotten that night on the palace grounds in Baronovia.

"We have to leave before the landlady comes looking for us," Dan said as he lovingly stroked her golden hair.

"I know," she agreed. Smiling, she gazed at him. He looked wonderful, she mused. Even though his clothes were rumpled and a two-day shadow of beard covered his face. There was something about his maleness that made her heart sing.

There was no future for them, she reminded herself as she straightened her hair and her blouse. She was the widow of the Baronovian ambassador and might only be in Washington for an undetermined length of time. Her future might be back in Baronovia.

She unconsciously compared Dan with her late husband. As Baronovia's ambassador, Rolande had always worried about his appearance and propriety. There was seldom a time that he wasn't fully clothed or without a tie. She felt guilty as she recalled the rare occasions he *had* taken off his tie on the nights when she'd longed for a human touch and had asked him to hold her before she slept. What would Rolande have thought if he could see her now?

"I have an idea," she said, forcing her thoughts to the present.

"Good. At the moment, I'm fresh out of ideas."

"My cousin, May. We could call her and ask her if she knows something that might lead us to Fritz and his friends."

"The duchess? What could she know about Fritz?"

"Maybe not Fritz, but about anyone who has been threatening the embassy. I understand that May and her father, the prince, were the targets of some discontented Baronovian nationalists two years ago. Maybe she knows if they're back and active."

"Yeah. I stupidly got myself involved in one of those attempts once—Wade Stevens, too. The guy was Gregor Petrov, the head of your former Baronovian Trade Commission. He's the guy who tried to take out Charlie and Mike Wheeler. Maybe he still holds a grudge."

"What happened to Petrov?"

"May used her connections to make sure he was deported, but the guy could be back by now. Or he might be in a position to influence someone like Fritz and his buddies to act for him. Let's go out to the car. If you know May's telephone number, I'll use my cell phone to call her."

Ten minutes later, Dan found that May had heard about Caroline's abduction through the servants' grapevine. He'd waited while she'd used another phone to call her father, Prince Alexis of Baronovia, to find out if someone was still trying to upset the diplomatic agreement between Baronovia and the United States. The answer shook him, but at least he had a definite lead.

"Gregor Petrov," he told Victoria. "I remember him. He claimed diplomatic immunity when it was discovered he was part of a plot to discredit Baronovia, but May used her position in the royal family to have the immunity removed."

"Where is Petrov now?"

"According to May, he was deported. She called home and was told Petrov is still in Baronovia, engaged in the liquor export business." Dan began to marvel at how neatly the pieces of the puzzle were coming together. "But he could have people he's working through here. I'm willing to bet they're those two foreign exchange students. And Fritz."

"Our brandy *is* highly regarded throughout the world," Victoria said thoughtfully. "Maybe Petrov owns the distributing outlet in Washington where Fritz goes to pick up the embassy's supply!" She paused to think. "The company's business name, if I remember correctly, is International Liquors."

"Then that's our answer!" Dan exploded. "I'm going after Petrov. If he's anywhere, he's at the liquor outlet. If not, maybe someone will know where he is."

Fearing that just the two of them wouldn't be enough to deal with finding Fritz, Victoria exclaimed, "I'm going with you. We need to get help, but who?"

Dan agreed. "One of the first lessons I learned during training was never to go into danger alone—always to have a backup." Whenever the chips were down, his fellow JAG officers were always there for each other. Even the JAG himself, Dan thought as he remembered the admiral's parting words to call if Dan needed him.

If ever there was a time to call in help, it was now. He'd play it close to his chest and ask May's husband, JAG Commander Wade Stevens, to help, but out of uniform.

He'd have to depend on Admiral Crowley to cover for the two of them if word of the caper came out.

As for Victoria, he thought as he gazed at the determined set to the lips he couldn't get enough of, the baby might need the comfort of her mother's arms when she was rescued, but Victoria needed someone to comfort her.

In the meantime, he had a couple of telephone calls to make.

INTERNATIONAL LIQUORS was listed in the D.C. business directory in the industrial side of eastern Washington, just the other side of the Beltway.

Dan, with Wade and a determined Victoria in the back seat, parked up the street from the ancient red-brick building that housed International Liquors. Outside wooden stairs indicated there was an office on the second floor. Sweet-smelling fumes spread by the afternoon breeze filled the air around the building.

"Smells good," Wade Stevens said, sniffing the air. "Wouldn't mind a shot or two of brandy about now."

"Not on the job," Dan said as he slid out of the car and surveyed the building. "If things work out the way I expect them to, I'll personally see you get a whole case."

Dan glanced at his watch. It was almost 5:00 p.m. If the export company followed usual local business hours, the work shift should have ended about half an hour ago.

"How about coming up here to the front seat, Victoria? If anything unusual happens, sound the horn—three short blasts. Wade, you go around to the back and see if there's a way to get inside the ground floor. I'll take the stairs up to the second floor and check it out. If I find anything unusual, I'll whistle three times. Got it?"

"No," she said as she slid across the seat. "I'm coming with you!"

Dan shrugged helplessly. If Victoria was determined to dog his footsteps, he'd learned by now that there was no way he could stop her. With her at his heels, he strode across the street and quietly made his way up the wooden stairs, wincing whenever a step creaked. He glanced over his shoulder and motioned Victoria to tread softly. Not to his surprise, he found an address above the door. The top half of the building had to be another business or...

Praying under his breath, he pulled out the gun he kept hidden in his belt beneath his jacket, took a deep breath and gently turned the door handle. The door was locked. With his gun at the ready he cast a warning glance over his shoulder at Victoria to step back and tried again. This time he kicked in the door.

A quick glance told him the interior was a one-room apartment. The windows had been painted over with dark-gray paint, a narrow bed was against the wall. What passed for a kitchen filled another wall. The only other furniture was a rickety wooden table and two chairs.

"Lydia! It *was* you!" Victoria cried as she rushed by Dan to the bed where Caroline lay, covered with her yellow afghan. "How could you have done this?"

"God has heard my prayers," Lydia said, tears rolling down her cheeks as she rushed to embrace Victoria. "Please forgive me! I was only trying to help."

"Help?" Dan strode into the room. "You call this helping?"

"Yes," she answered. "Soon after the party started, I came back to the nursery to check on the baby. I found Fritz there, taking Caroline out of her crib. She'd started to cry. I couldn't let him take her. I argued with him. He had a gun. I told him if he took the baby, he had to take me, too. He was angry, but he finally told me to hurry. I carried Caroline. I gave her her little yellow teddy bear and wrapped her in the afghan.''

By now, to Dan's chagrin, Victoria was sobbing along with Lydia. "Why didn't you scream for help?"

"There was so much noise at the party. I could even hear it upstairs. I hoped that someone would see us and stop us before we drove away in the limousine. Will you ever forgive me?"

"Of course," Victoria said as she took Lydia in her arms. "When you've been so good to the baby, how can I not?"

Dan left the two women to comfort each other, went to the outside stair landing and whistled three times.

Wade Stevens was already bounding up the stairs, gun at the ready. "I was getting worried. What's up?"

"We found Lydia and Caroline, they're okay, thank God. Seems Lydia insisted that Fritz, her nephew who took the baby, take her along, too. Wouldn't take no for an answer, just like Victoria. Gotta tell you," Dan said, his heart slowly grinding to its normal beat, "these Baronovian women are the kind of women you don't want to tangle with."

"Tell me about it." Wade grinned. "I married one. I guess you won't be needing me anymore." He put his gun back in his belt and paused before turning away. "This might not be the time or place to tell you this, pal, but we are good friends, right?"

"Right." Dan eyed his friend warily. "Sounds as if you have something to say. Spit it out."

"I know about your relationship to Caroline. May told me," Wade said under his breath. "I would have helped you in any case, but that's besides the point. The point is, May is very concerned about Victoria's position in all of this."

"I know." Back down to earth, Dan nodded. "Once it became clear I had to be Caroline's father, I've considered Victoria's situation with every waking moment and with every breath I take. I don't apologize for having made love to Victoria, in case you're interested," he added defiantly. "I don't think she would apologize, either. I'm only sorry I didn't find out about the baby until now."

"And now?"

"I'm going to get out of Victoria's life as soon as I get her, Lydia and the baby back to the embassy. She has a duty to her country. I'm sure she won't turn her back on it. As for me," he said ruefully, "I'm not about to become a trophy husband. I'm a JAG lawyer, and I'd like to keep it that way. My sense of duty and honor isn't confined to working hours."

"And what does Victoria say about that?"

"I haven't asked," Dan said. "She's had enough heartache to last a lifetime."

Wade nodded compassionately. "Let me know if there's anything I can do, okay?"

"Sure. You'll be the first to know."

Wade grinned and bounded down the stairs.

Dan took a deep breath and went back inside the apartment, closing the door behind him.

Just then, as if on cue, Caroline awakened and rolled over. "Mama!"

"Yes, my darling," Victoria said as she reached for the baby. Held-back tears streamed down her cheeks, this time with joy. "Mama's here."

Dan forced back his own tears as he watched Victoria hold the baby close. Men don't cry? Like hell, he thought with a lump in his throat. Nothing would ever top the satisfaction of seeing Victoria and his daughter reunited. Nor would anything be more rewarding than to see the smiles beneath the tears on the face of the woman he loved.

Not even bringing Fritz to justice would top this.

Chapter Fourteen

"You wanted to see me, sir?" At attention, his eyes fixed on a spot behind his commanding officer's right ear, Dan waited for what he was sure was coming next. It was a trick he'd mastered long ago to keep from meeting the admiral's eyes when the going got rough. Crowley had to have heard about the role he'd played in the return of little Caroline Bernard.

Judging from Crowley's frown, Dan's extracurricular activities hadn't left the man happy.

Crowley studied Dan for a long, uncomfortable moment before he finally spoke. "At ease, Commander."

Dan relaxed and put his hands behind his back. "Aye, aye, sir."

Crowley waited just long enough to make Dan wonder if he'd also heard about his fellow lawyer Wade Stevens's role in the baby's rescue.

"Do you mind telling me just what in the hell this is all about?"

Dan followed Crowley's pointed finger. A huge wicker basket tied with a yellow ribbon rested on a table. In the basket and nestled in cellophane cuttings, there were at least a dozen bottles of brandy. Each carved brown glass bottle was clearly labeled Baronovia's Finest. A tray of dried fruits and nuts was tucked in one side of the basket.

Surprised at the turn the meeting was taking, Dan blinked. "Who sent it, sir?"

"The card said, Compliments of the Baronovian Embassy. It also said, In Gratitude for the Efforts of Your Staff. Now," Crowley added dryly, "just what staff do you think the card was referring to, Commander? You?"

Dan managed a straight face. "Probably, sir. It's a long story." He crossed his fingers behind his back. If Crowley knew about Wade Stevens's role in rescuing Caroline, he was ignoring it.

"Well," Crowley said as he ambled over to the basket and picked out a date, "if the story is that long, maybe I would be better off not hearing it?"

"Maybe not, sir," Dan said gratefully. Clearly, although Crowley had offered to help if needed, the man was better off not knowing the details of how Fritz had walked into the trap Dan had set for him. Or how he'd "persuaded" Fritz to come back to the embassy for the ambassador to deal with instead of making the incident public.

"I assume you've taken care of the young damsel in distress?"

"Yes, sir."

Crowley sat down on the corner of his desk and gazed at Dan quizzically. "Would there be a marriage in your future?"

"No, sir." Dan had learned early in his JAG career never to volunteer any more information than was necessary to keep his superior officer happy. Besides, from the way things looked, he could be five years away from acquiring a wife.

"In that case, Commander, is it safe to assume your leave is over and that you're back on board?"

"Yes, sir."

"Good." Crowley bit into the date, chewed thoughtfully, then reached for another. "Dismissed, and close the door behind you."

Dan eyed the gift basket warily and made for the door counting his blessings. The only person that grateful for his involvement in helping to recover Caroline had to be Victoria's father.

As for the gift itself, Dan had a growing suspicion there had been another message there in addition to the ambassador's thanks.

With Fritz and his two buddies now in the embassy's tender loving care, and a distraught Lydia on her way home to Baronovia, the case was apparently, as far as he was concerned, over. What did bother him was he hadn't had a chance to tell Victoria he would never forget her.

Until Victoria looked him square in his eyes and told him she was happy to remain a widow, their relationship, at least as far as he was concerned, *wasn't* over after all. He hadn't been able to walk away from her when she needed him, and he wasn't going to walk away from her now.

He reached for the phone.

VICTORIA GENTLY removed the baby's finger from the corner of her rosebud mouth and tucked the yellow afghan around her sleeping daughter. Instead of turning away, she stood at the side of the crib and, deep in thought, counted her blessings.

She was grateful to Dan for finding Caroline.

She was grateful to her father for allowing Dan to take part in the search. And even more grateful for the gracious way he had received and thanked Dan on their return.

But, she thought sadly as she stood there, would gratitude be enough to see her through the lonely days and nights ahead of her?

What she yearned for were nights with Dan holding her in his arms and making love to her the way he had so long ago. To warm her, to make her senses shout and to send her soaring to the stars. To satisfy the longings that tormented her more and more as time went by.

She sighed, and with a loving look went back to her own room—only to be confronted by the empty king-size bed.

Images of herself with Dan beside her overwhelmed her.

Faced with the knowledge of the lonely years ahead, she knew she couldn't go on this way—lying to herself. She sank onto the bed. How would she be able to go on alone?

The phone rang.

TWO HOURS later, Dan opened his apartment door to Victoria. After their telephone conversation, he didn't intend to inquire why she had asked to come to his apartment. The miracle was that she had.

"How did you get here?"

"I took a taxi. My own car is too well-known at home."

"Thank you for coming," he said gratefully as he drew her inside. "I was hoping we would have private time to say goodbye."

Dan's heart ached for Victoria and the mental turmoil he sensed she must have gone through before she'd decided to come here to say goodbye. His heart also ached for himself, he thought as he bit back the words he wanted to say.

Dan closed the door behind Victoria. "May I?" he asked as he drew her raincoat off her shoulders. She was wearing a woolen pantsuit and a green silk blouse that buttoned to her chin. Drops of rainwater clung to her hair. "Hang on a minute while I get something to dry you off." He brought her a towel from the bathroom and helped her off with her jacket.

"I know why you're here," he told her, "but be-

fore you get started, there's something I wanted to
tell you.''

"There's something I wanted to tell you, too,"
she said, her face covered and her voice muffled
under the towel.

Dan's heart plunged. He'd been right, she was
trying to find a polite way to say goodbye. "Coffee,
tea? It'll warm you up.''

"Coffee, please." She smiled as she emerged
from under the towel. "I've actually learned to like
coffee since I came to your country.''

Dan cringed inside as she put distance between
them. *His country?* Was that her way of showing
him the impossible distance between them?

He busied himself at the sink measuring fresh coffee beans, grinding them and filling the coffeemaker
with water. Anything to stall for time, he thought
ruefully. He'd never been good at saying goodbye.
"Cream, sugar?''

He turned to look at Victoria. To his surprise, she
was curled up on the couch watching him in a way
that sent shivers racing up his spine.

"Look, Victoria, we can't go on this way," he
said, raking his fingers through his hair in his frustration. "I know this is hard on you, so why don't
we cut to the chase? If you've come here to thank
me, then you're welcome. It was no big deal—I
helped because my heart was in it. If you've come
to say goodbye, well, I guess I expect that, too.''

"You do?''

"Yes. I promised you I'd never bother you again. Seeing you, knowing you, makes that promise hard to keep." He smiled ruefully. "One way or another, I guess I've found out everything I wanted to know. So…" He took a deep breath and held out his hand. "Goodbye."

"No goodbye, not until we talk." At the desolate look in Dan's eyes, a fire grew in Victoria's heart. How could he not know how much she cared for him? How could he not know her life would never be the same now that she'd found him? She sniffed at the pungent scent of the brewing coffee. "And not before I have that cup of coffee you offered me. I like mine black.

"You must think I've lost my mind," she went on with a wry smile. "Actually, I think I lost it on the night we first met."

Dan dropped his hand to his side. The woman smiling at him was someone he wasn't sure he'd known before. Instead of the sweet and unsure person she'd seemed to be at their first meeting, or the frightened woman she'd been each time they'd met lately, she was self-assured and assertive.

It was as if she'd taken a giant step from the nineteenth century into the twenty-first. And, like her royal cousin May, she had blossomed into a radiant and confident woman. What really surprised him was that, in spite of the fact they'd been as close as a man and a woman could be, she still could keep him guessing.

Dan swallowed hard, poured two cups of coffee and set one on the coffee table for Victoria. "You think you've lost your mind or are you sure?" he asked cautiously, afraid to hope she had another reason for coming here this afternoon. "You know I lost mine the night I met you again at the Stevenses' housewarming."

Victoria sensed from the closed look on Dan's face he was expecting her to try to let him down easily. A week ago, her loyalty and gratitude to her husband's memory would have compelled her to do exactly that. Recent events had not only miraculously changed her life, they had forced her to take a look at her future. First, she had to be sure of Dan and the way he really felt about her.

"But it isn't your mind we have to worry about, is it?" She sipped her coffee and studied him over the rim of her cup. Did he really love her, or had she been just another challenge in his life? Was she only a puzzle he'd come across almost two years ago and was determined to solve now?

She set down her cup and plunged to the heart of the matter. "My family knows Caroline is your child."

Dan choked on his coffee and came up sputtering. "You told them?"

"I didn't have to. My parents always knew Caroline couldn't be Rolande's. After meeting you and comparing you to the picture of Caroline, my father asked me last night if you were her natural father.

When I said yes, he told me the resemblance between you and the baby was so strong, it had to be the truth. He just hadn't known the name of the man who fathered her, and neither did I. Not until you and I met again.''

Dan's face blanched as he remembered the gift basket, and the uneasy sensation that it carried a dual message. Suddenly it all began to make sense. It was Basil Esterhazy's subtle way of thanking him for bringing Caroline home. And his way of signaling he wouldn't stand in their way. What kind of man was he to leave Victoria to face her family alone?

"My God, Victoria! Are you okay? I should have been there for you!'' Dan wanted to take Victoria in his arms and apologize for not finding her the morning after they'd made passionate love in the palace gardens. But for some reason he couldn't.

"I'm fine,'' she said, praying Dan would claim her now. Instead, he paced the floor.

"And now that you've found me again—do you hate me?'' Dan said, clenching his hands, afraid to touch her, afraid she would blame him for leaving her behind when he returned to the United States after the wedding.

"I couldn't hate you,'' she said wistfully. "I've already told you, it was more my fault than yours. After you left, you were a dream I held close to me at night,'' she went on, "but, for the sake of my marriage vows, I never dared to dream you would become real.''

"You're saying?" His heart leaped in his throat. He'd been so near and yet so far from finding the one woman he wanted to spend the rest of his life with. He steeled himself to hear her say she'd chosen to return to Baronovia alone.

"So you've made a decision?" Dan had to force himself not to reach out to Victoria. To show her how much he loved her. To convince her that if he had his way, there would be no choice at all. She belonged to him.

"Whatever I decide," Victoria went on, "the one thing I ask is that Rolande always be regarded as Caroline's father. He always loved her as if she were his own."

"I'm not sure just what you're asking of *me*," Dan said, his frustration almost getting the better of him, "but I know it's not fair for me to ask you to choose between me and your child. Or to make the choice for you."

"I know," she said, her luminous eyes looking into his. "But first, I have to know how you really feel about me. I know we wanted each other that night at the palace, but do you love me now?"

How could he tell Victoria he loved her? Saying the right words was one thing, the result of the words would be another. At the thought of giving her up, a hollow dread filled him. Life would be empty without her, but how could he ask her to choose him? To live the life of a spouse of a naval lawyer without the luxurious trappings she'd been accustomed to all her life?

"I haven't had a chance to tell you before now," he said as he realized he couldn't give her up. That there was more than a physical bond between them. That he loved her for her courage, her honesty and her loyalty to those she cared about.

"I think I fell in love with you back in Baronovia, I just didn't know it," he said. "I looked for you the very next day, but I couldn't find you. I thought I would never see you again. In fact," he added wryly, "I wasn't even sure I recognized you when we met again. It wasn't until I held you in my arms at the housewarming party that I suspected you were my mystery lady."

"Do you really love me? Or was I just another woman, a passing challenge at a time when romance was in the air?"

"I'd show you how much I care, if I could," he said as he drew away to keep from gathering her in his arms.

"I've made my choice, or I wouldn't be here now," Victoria said gently, a smile covering her face. "But there's a catch. If you really want me, you must agree to honor my request that Rolande be thought of as Caroline's father."

Dan thought of the moment when he'd compared Caroline's photograph with his own as a small boy and first realized the baby was his flesh and blood. And the pride he'd felt at knowing he was her father.

Could he, in all honesty, not claim his daughter? "I've heard and seen enough to know blood ties don't necessarily make a father," he said, "so I will go along with your request." He finally gave in to the need to tenderly brush her cheeks, kiss the tip of her nose. "She bears his name and from what you've told me, he was a caring and loving father to Caroline. I couldn't bring myself to embarrass his memory, not when he did so much for you," he said as he took a deep breath. "When Caroline grows older, if you like, we can tell her the truth."

"Thank heaven you are such an honorable man," Victoria whispered, her eyes brimming with love for Dan. She raised her lips for his kiss. "I love you for being so understanding."

"That's all you love me for?"

"Well," she said with a wicked grin, "there *is* this..." She slowly unbuttoned his shirt and eased it off his shoulders. When he tensed, she ran her hands over his chest and teased the nipples that hardened under her touch. "It's been so long," she murmured. "I'm not sure I remember just what I need to do to please you."

"You're off to a great start. My turn," he said as he took his time unbuttoning the green blouse that matched her tantalizing eyes. He kissed each inch of her exposed warm and sweet-scented flesh and finally reached behind her to unfasten her bra. He drew it from her shoulders. "Beautiful," he said softly as he buried his head between her aching breasts. "Can we take the rest of your clothes off?"

"Only if you take yours off, too," she said, hardly recognizing herself as the woman who had wistfully watched from the outside as life had passed her by. "I have a lot of catching up to do."

Clothes flew off in a flurry and fell around them as he carried her to his bedroom and gently dropped her on the bed.

"I need you," she murmured. "I need you now." Straining with desire, she tried to get closer, to show him how much she wanted him to make her his, to satisfy the longings she'd lived with too long.

"You're sure about this, sweetheart?" she heard him murmur as his breath brushed her ear and he kissed every inch of her heated skin.

"I'm sure," she said as he reached for the place she yearned for him to fill. She put her arms around his neck, and joyfully opened herself to him.

"Lovely," she heard him whisper as he sensuously ran his hand over her body. She strained into his hand and felt she would burst into flames if he didn't finish what they had begun. This was the man she'd dreamed about for almost two years. This was the only man to have made love to her, and the only man she wanted to make love to for the rest of her life.

She felt his hard arousal against her hip as he ran his hands down to her waist, her thighs and lower still. Desire swelled and raced through her like flames. She couldn't get enough of the taste of him, the scent of him, the sound of his low voice murmuring love words. Until now, he'd only been a dream. Now he was real.

When he slid into her and ran his tongue over her hardened nipples, she felt as if she would surely melt into a mound of molten wax. "Oh, my," she said as waves of sensation sent her soaring.

"Yes, oh, my," he echoed, tender laughter in his voice. "Hold on, I've only just begun to show you how I feel about you, sweetheart."

Victoria's breath caught in her throat; she was afraid to take a deep breath. Her senses caught fire as his lips continued to tantalize her until, aching for more, she arched under his touch. He held her so close that she felt almost as if he were a second skin.

Bursts of pleasure exploded within her as waves of feeling swept her. Pleasure heightened when he tensed and shouted his release.

"Only with you," she murmured when he finally kissed her one more time, slid to his side and gathered her to him. "Only with you."

TWO HOURS later, Victoria awakened when she felt Dan stir. "What?"

"Time to take you home, sweetheart," he said as he dropped a kiss on her nose. "If I have my way, there's going to be lots more of this unless you have another plan in mind," he added as he outlined her sensitive lips with a tender forefinger. "I have great plans for the future and they all include you.'' He laughed as he slid out of bed and pulled her up beside him. ''Have I ever told you about my five-year plan?''

''*Our* five-year plan?'' she amended with a shrewd question in her sparkling green eyes.

''Don't ask,'' he laughed into her throat. ''Besides, it looks as if my plan may have kicked in eighteen months ago. It's just taken me a little while to realize it.''

She struggled to open her eyes. ''Tell me about it now or take me back to bed.''

Epilogue

Six Months Later

May Stevens, glowing with happiness for her cousin, smiled at her friend Charlie Wheeler. "I was afraid I would never see this day," she said cheerfully. "Victoria and Dan had so many odds to overcome, but in the end..."

"We've all been lucky, haven't we?" Charlie agreed.

"How's the new baby, Michaela? I know you and Mike wanted a girl."

"Great." Charlie beamed. "For the first time since Mike and I got married, Jake didn't want to tag along with us. He insisted he would stay home and take care of his little sister!"

May patted her tummy and laughed. "My doctor has told me I'm going to have twins! Wade is beside himself with pride. As if I had nothing to do with it!"

"Men!" Charlie agreed with a satisfied glance at her husband, Mike, the lone usher without a uniform who waited at the chapel door.

Beside him stood two other players in the O'Hara-Esterhazy-Bernard wedding.

"That makes two JAG officers who married women from the Baronovian royal family and brought them home to the States," Admiral Crowley dryly observed to Patrick O'Hara as he waited outside the chapel for the traditional gauntlet ceremony to begin. Around him, wedding guests were gathered waiting expectantly for the new bride and groom. "There's something to be said about a uniform, right?"

"Right," Patrick agreed. "Of course, if the boys had been in the sub service, they probably would have brought back the whole damn country of Baronovia instead of its women."

Crowley laughed. "Or if they'd been Navy Seals," he added. "Still, there's obviously nothing wrong with belonging to the JAG Corps. Lawyers seem to be a pretty enterprising bunch," he said modestly. He refrained from pointing out that he was a lawyer as well as a former Seal.

"Maybe so," O'Hara returned, with a sidelong glance at the admiral. "Still, the navy's the navy, thank God."

"I'll drink to that. With men like your nephew under my command, I've had to hoist one or two to keep my nerves calm myself," Crowley laughed.

"Me, too," O'Hara sighed dramatically. "I can hardly wait for the reception party." O'Hara looked around and lowered his voice. "I made sure they have plenty of Guinness, you know."

"God bless the Irish, I'll drink to that. Now, if your nephew Dan could only stay out of trouble…"

"Has Dan ever told you about his five-year plan?" Pat O'Hara asked.

"No," Crowley said dryly. "To tell the truth, nothing the man could come up with would surprise me. Of course, now that he's won his bride, maybe I can relax. Or," he asked cautiously, "are there any more Baronovian women in the family?"

"Not that I know of. Ah, there's the organ," O'Hara said as the wedding recessional music sounded and the bride and groom appeared in the doorway of the chapel. "Now comes the interesting part."

Eight JAG officers dressed in immaculate white-and-gold uniforms lined up at the entrance to the navy chapel. Sunlight shone off their ceremonial swords and gold braid as they hoisted the swords into the air to create an arch under which the bride and groom would pass.

A cheer went up when the happy bride and groom started out the door. In her simple off-white silk gown Victoria smiled shyly, her arm entwined with Dan's. A diamond wedding band encircled her wedding-ring finger. A wreath of tiny pink roses circled her now-auburn hair. Around her throat she wore a single strand of pearls. Her first wedding had taken place in a large church with Prince Alexis and the extended Baron family in attendance. She'd gone through the motions then, but today—today, she felt like singing.

Today had to be the second-happiest day of her life, she thought as she smiled up at her new husband. A husband she had chosen for herself and whose touch sent her heart soaring.

The first had been that night two years ago in a palace garden when she'd given her heart away to Dan as they'd made love in a gazebo under a crescent moon. She hadn't been able to see him clearly that night because of the mist that had swirled around them, but she saw him clearly today.

He was handsome and tall in his white dress uniform. The dimple in his chin was more pronounced than ever as he smiled down at her, a glowing promise in his eyes. His arm pulled her closer.

"Happy, Mrs. O'Hara?"

"Happy, Mr. O'Hara. And this time," she whispered with a saucy smile, "I'm never, ever going to let you go."

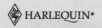

**Start the New Year off regally with
a two-book duo from**

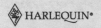

*A runaway prince and his horse-wrangling
lookalike confuse and confound
the citizens of Ranger Springs, Texas, in*

♛A ROYAL
TWIST
by
Victoria Chancellor

Rodeo star Hank McCauley just happened to be a dead ringer
for His Royal Highness Prince Alexi of Belegovia—who had just
taken off from his tour of Texas with a spirited, sexy waitress.
Now, Hank must be persuaded by the very prim-and-proper
Lady Gwendolyn Reed to pose as the prince until the lost leader
is found. But could she turn the cowpoke into a Prince
Charming? And could Hank persuade Lady "Wendy" to let
down her barriers so that he could have her, body and soul?

Don't miss:

THE PRINCE'S COWBOY DOUBLE
January 2003

Then read Prince Alexi's story in:

THE PRINCE'S TEXAS BRIDE
February 2003

Available at your favorite retail outlet.

COOPER'S CORNER

Cooper's Corner continues in February 2003 with

FOR THE LOVE OF MIKE!
by Muriel Jensen

Check-in: The cozy Twin Oaks B and B—the perfect retreat for single dad Michael Flynn to kick back with his two young daughters...and their St. Bernard. Single mom Colleen O'Connor had the same idea for her and her two little boys...and their Siamese cat. Bad combination!

Checkout: Soon Mike and Colleen found themselves fighting...their attraction!

HARLEQUIN®

Makes any time special®

Visit us at www.cooperscorner.com

CC-CNM7

eHARLEQUIN.com

Becoming an eHarlequin.com member is easy,
fun and **FREE!** Join today to enjoy great benefits:

- **Super savings** on all our books, including
  members-only discounts and offers!

- Enjoy **exclusive online reads**—FREE!

- Info, tips and **expert advice** on writing
  your own romance novel.

- FREE romance **newsletters,**
  customized by you!

- Find out the latest on your
  favorite authors.

- Enter to win exciting **contests
  and promotions!**

- Chat with other members in our
  community message boards!

**Plus, we'll send you 2 FREE Internet-exclusive
eHarlequin.com books (no strings!)
just to say thanks for joining us online.**

To become a member,
visit www.eHarlequin.com today!

HARLEQUIN®

AMERICAN *Romance*®

Bestselling author
Muriel Jensen
kicks off

MILLIONAIRE, MONTANA

beginning in January 2003 with
JACKPOT BABY

Welcome to Millionaire, Montana, where twelve lucky
townspeople have won a multimillion-dollar jackpot.
And where one millionaire in particular has just…
found a baby on her doorstep.

The excitement continues with:

BIG-BUCKS BACHELOR by Leah Vale
on-sale February 2003

SURPRISE INHERITANCE by Charlotte Douglas
on-sale March 2003

FOUR-KARAT FIANCÉE by Sharon Swan
on-sale April 2003

PRICELESS MARRIAGE by Bonnie Gardner
on-sale May 2003

FORTUNE'S TWINS by Kara Lennox
on-sale June 2003

Available at your favorite retail outlet.

HARLEQUIN®
Makes any time special®

Coming in February 2003 from

HARLEQUIN®

AMERICAN *Romance®*

BIG-BUCKS BACHELOR
by
Leah Vale

The latest book in the scintillating six-book series,

MILLIONAIRE, MONTANA

Welcome to Millionaire, Montana, where twelve lucky
townspeople have won a multimillion-dollar jackpot.
And where one millionaire in particular has just...
caught himself a fake fiancée.

MILLIONAIRE, MONTANA continues with

SURPRISE INHERITANCE
by Charlotte Douglas,
on sale March 2003.

Available at your favorite retail outlet.

HARLEQUIN®
Makes any time special®

Visit us at www.eHarlequin.com

HARBBB